blue
talk
&love

Mecca
Jamilah
Sullivan

For more information contact:
Riverdale Avenue Books
5676 Riverdale Avenue
Riverdale, NY 10471.

www.riverdaleavebooks.com

Design by www.formatting4U.com
Cover design by Hanifah Walidah
Cover art by Mirlande Jean-Gilles: "Girl With the Big 'Fro"

Digital ISBN 9781626011618
Print ISBN 9781626011625

First Edition March 2015

Stories in Blue Talk and Love first appeared in:

"Wolfpack," *Best New Writing 2010*, Hopewell Publishing, 2010

"Blue Talk and Love," *American Fiction: Best Previously Unpublished Short Stories by Emerging Writers*, vol.12, New Rivers Press, 2012

"Snow Fight," *Baby Remember My Name: New Queer Girl Fiction*, ed. Michelle Tea. Carroll & Graf, 2007

"Powder and Smoke," *Bloom: Queer Fiction, Art, Poetry and More,* Spring 2005

"A Strange People," *Crab Orchard Review* 14.1, Winter, 2008

"Saturday," *Lumina* 6, Spring 2006

"Sererie," *Callaloo*, Spring, 2010

"A Magic of Bags," *From Where We Sit: Black Writers Write Black Youth,* Tiny Satchel Press, 2011

"Ivy," *Baobab: South African Journal of New Writing,* Fall 2009

"Adale," *X-24: Unlcassified*, Lubin & Kleyner, 2007

"Friday, Field Trip Day," *Philadelphia Stories online*, 2007

"Ruídos ," *Minnesota Review*, Summer 2010

"The Anvil," Feminist Studies Vol. 40 no. 2, Fall 2014.

"Wall Women," *Woman's Work: An Anthology*, Girlchild Press, 2010

Contents

Wolfpack

For the New Jersey Four

This story is for Patreese Johnson, Terrain Dandridge, Venice Brown, and Renata Hill, who, in 2007, received prison sentences ranging from three and a half to eleven years for the alleged felony gang assault of a man who threatened to rape them in New York City's West Village. The story is also for Chenese Loyal, Lania Daniels, and Khamysha Coates, who were offered plea bargains in the same case. The women have been known collectively as the New Jersey Seven.

Verniece

This is a story that matters, so listen. I'ma tell it. The summer my words were snatched away, the weatherman on Channel Nine kept promising a heat wave. Had me dreaming of days curled up under the dust and rattle of the AC with my son, Anthony Jesús, and nights out in the Village with my lady and our squad. It was the summer after high school graduation, and a heat wave woulda left my mother too drained to

1

hassle me about my life, my weight, and my plans. None of her muttering: "What you fi do, Verniece, sit at home with that girl, getting big as this house while your baby starve? Yu na have plan?" My plan was I was gonna go to college to major in Astronomy, back when I bothered with a future tense. When I told my mother this, she usually grunted. "No, yu nah gwan waste my money or yours, studying some devilment 'bout birthdays and signs." She would sigh her anger, sucking my dreams from me like the gristle from a chicken bone.

I looked forward to sweating it out that summer, gathering words for that fight. But the damn heat wave never came. Days, weekends, weeks, months passed, and nothing. I started to imagine myself leaping into the television with the weatherman and snatching the gray-speckled rug off his head, just to show him how it felt to have small hopes taken away. But that was not my spirit back then, before my words left me. I was patient, quiet. I waited.

I don't remember everything that happened that night, but the things that came before—I know those like my skin. Those stories—the ones that make what happened to us matter—are not about a man who tore into our summer and broke us. Those stories are about us—about me and my lady, our homegirls, and our son. Who we are and who we were, who we might never be again.

Before they took my words away, it was me and Luna and Anthony Jesús, plus my mother, when she wanted to act right. Even when she didn't, our family was the proudest thing I had. We were not like the teen pregnancy stories you see on television. I wanted

Anthony Jesús as much as anyone ever wanted anything—a million times more than I ever wanted some man. Truth be told, my mother was happy to learn a baby was coming, too. Seeing Luna and me together and so strong for two years made her panic, started her in early on those things that middle-aged mothers go through—hassling me about when I'd find a husband, worrying endlessly about growing old on God's Green Earth with no grandbabies to care for. Sometimes, when the bookshelf buckled or a doorknob came loose, she would take an Olympic breath and sigh out: "Yu know we need a man in the family, with yuah papa gone now."

I would get up quickly from wherever I was and fix whatever was broken. Then I would remind her— silently, in my mind—that my father had died a decade ago, and had never been the handyman type in life. *Be careful what you wish for*, my fantasy self would say. I knew it wasn't a son-in-law, or even grandchildren, that she wanted. What she wanted was a different kind of daughter. If I had come to her at any point in high school to tell her I'd sworn off pussy and decided to go celibate, become a nun, she woulda flown to the church, tithed her whole pension, and sung the choir off the altar with the force of her gratitude. Her problem with me had nothing to do with motherhood. It was about womanhood, and which kind of woman I would be. In my mind, I told her all about herself. But in real life, I said nothing. Just counted the weeks till Luna and I had saved enough money to pay her cousin for his Y chromosomes.

Luna went to school and worked two jobs that summer, while Anthony Jesús and I kept each other

3

company, held each other down in my mother's house. Luna would come home from her afternoon gig at the Pretty Look nail salon on Bloomfield Ave with soul food dinners for all of us, my mother included. Every time, my mother refused. She would look at the bag in Luna's hand, all grease-heavy and smelling good. She'd breathe in the smell and you could see the want on her face. But she'd purse her lips, pat her stomach, and say "M-mm, no. Me nah feel settle," and turn back to her room. Then I'd hear her, late at night, muttering to herself as she crept to the kitchen, rifling through the leftovers, "Just fi likkle pick."

Luna didn't let my mother get to her. She just hid her hurt and kept trying. She sang to me and the baby whenever we needed it, brought home bootleg telenovela DVDs whenever I asked, and told me my body was her favorite place on earth. Her lips were like sponges just wrung free of cool water, perfect on Anthony Jesús's cheeks, perfect anywhere on me.

We weren't sweating what my mother—or anyone else—had to say back then. I still had the words I thought would protect me from everyone's opinions, keep me doing alright in the world. I found those words the same day I found our son's name, and I thought both would hold me down forever. That was a year before that night in the Village, four weeks after I pissed pink on the EPT strip. My mother dragged me to Saint Anthony's, eager to have me "put likkle face" in, let the old church ladies see me again before my belly started to show. Her face was a bright mix of shame and glee—happy about the baby, sad about me, and so I was sure the day would be miserable. I hated church usually—the slowness of it, the meanness of the women, the sour-breathed gossip and the eyes raking you down when you went for communion, looking to see if you'd put on weight. My father never went to church, and when I asked him why once, sometime in the third grade, he told me that being black and awake in America was enough of a double-bind for him; he had no interest in an afterlife that promised more of the same. I didn't know exactly what he meant, but it sounded right to me. I hustled my way out of going to church as often as I could, and when I did go I did my best to send my mind away.

But the day my words came to me, I couldn't get out of going. And so I sat in the pew with my mother, letting the music pass the time as always, thinking about eating fried wantons with Luna when I got home. But at the end of the service, something happened. The closing hymn that day did something— took me from the shaggy pew where I was sitting, made me forget the press of my too-tight pantyhose, my mother's hips against mine. I can't remember what the song was called, but I remember how the lyrics surprised me. They were not the usual tired mess about a man in the sky who said *Do This* and *Don't Do That* in a language nobody understood, or a ghost who played truth or dare games with your soul. There was no double bind, no damned-if-you-do, no one saying what to do or be. The lyrics were just a name. And just like any word changes shape when you say it long enough, this word changed, too. Eventually I stopped hearing everything around it, and the name meant something simple: *You are a person. God loves you. That's it.* So I got up and I left the pew, but I took those words and the feeling with me. I put all that into our baby's name—Anthony Jesús—and let the past sag to the ground like a churchlady's scowl.

For the next few months, I made those words a gate behind my ears: *We are people. God loves us. That's it.* I repeated the words in my mind wherever I went. Whatever was going to get to me had to fit through those words first. Those words kept me going with my head up when I walked around the city with my homegirl LaShanya—a slim, pretty, light-skinned type girl with a long auburn weave. But after I found those words, I almost didn't care. I could walk with my homegirl and just be with her and laugh. When I went around Newark holding Luna's hand or pushing the baby, those words kept the frowns and pointing fingers at a distance, and made it so I almost didn't see the looks people gave us. By August, I thought I had gotten good at a new kind of hearing, a new kind of seeing—the kind that made no room for people's chuckles and the stares. I thought I had learned how to walk in the world just feeling like a person, no matter who else was around. But the night my words fell away, I learned I was wrong.

It was a Saturday night, and I remember the moon looking bright, like the white tip of a freshly-manicured nail. It was hot, finally, and Luna had gotten off from the Pretty Look early, so we went with our girls to the Village to relax, do us, enjoy the summer. We were rolling deeper than usual that night—there were seven of us altogether: me, Luna, LaShanya (who we all call Sha), and our girl TaRonne and her woman, plus two of Sha's friends—a rich, Jersey City girl named Margina and a brownskinned femme named Angelique, with dreadlocks and an eyebrow ring. Sha collected friends like jewelry, picking them up whenever they caught her eye, valuing them enough, but never crying too hard over the occasional loss. The people she brought around usually fell right in with most of us. They were Sha's people, and so they were cool with me.

TaRonne's teacher girlfriend, Arya, must have been upset about something, because she snorted like a sick dog every time TaRonne talked on the ride to the Village. TaRonne treated Arya's attitude like how a little kid treats a video game, pushing random buttons and giggling at the response. "Arya's in a bad mood," she announced to all of us from the back seat. "She don't understand why we always walk around in the Vil when we could be sipping sherry with other *young professionals* like her." Arya huffed and looked out the window. "Nah, I know what it is," TaRonne said after a few seconds. "She's just worn out from being so intelligent, and accomplished, and fine. It ain't easy being a dream come true." She squeezed Arya's waist and let her head fall onto her chest. Arya sighed and ran her hand over TaRonne's fade, pushing her own cheeks toward the window to hide her smile.

We parked on West Street and walked up to the pier on Christopher to drink Coronas and watch the rich people's lights flicker on the other side of the Hudson. When we got to our regular bench, Sha turned to Margina and asked if she knew anyone who lived in one of those apartments. "I just want to know who my neighbors will be when I blow up," Sha explained, crossing her legs and fanning her dress out behind her on the bench. Margina leaned her back against the railing and said, "Um, I don't think I know anyone there," her voice all nervous and small. I decided then that I liked Margina—she was quiet like me. But TaRonne liked to make waves.

"Right, right," she said. "I guess you not in the habit of mingling with Daddy's tenants. I know how it is." Margina turned the color of Pepto Bismol and tried to sound hood. "Nah, it's not even like that, yo" she said. Then she gave an awkward smile, crossed her legs, and looked down at her shirt.

We could all tell the little girl was feeling TaRonne, but Arya wasn't bothered at all—she was out for fun. She uncapped a bottle of beer for Margina and raised her own. "To new experiences!" she said. Then she tongued TaRonne down right there, hands palming TaRonne's skull like a basketball, her eyes wide open and staring dead at Margina. The couple's love tiff must have dissolved by then, because they didn't stop kissing till Luna busted out in her jingle-bell chuckle. Then the rich girl went from pink to purple, and turned her face back toward Jersey. Luna put her arms around my waist and we threw our heads back, drinking our laughter like raindrops.

That was the last thing I remember before the man showed up—all of us laughing, kissing, feeling at home in the night. I keep that moment high up on a shelf in my mind now, in a row of important times I do not want to forget: the first time I saw my baby smile, the day my father gave me a toy telescope for no reason other than it made him think of me. The day I found my words-- the words that left me, in a second, for a lifetime, that night on the pavement.

Now that my words are gone and I have nothing but time to think back, I remember another moment that belongs on that list, too. It's another story that matters, even if it only matters to me. It was months before that night in August, but I see it clear as yesterday. Anthony Jesús hadn't been born yet, but he was one of our plans, along with my astronomy and Luna's zoology and a tall house in the suburbs with mango smoothies always in the freezer. Luna was reading on the sofa while I sat at my father's old desk, making flashcards for a Spanish test. The day was so still it almost seemed fake. For hours, it seemed like the only things moving were the little bits of dust that floated in the strip of light between my mother's curtains, tumbling slowly over themselves like cells under a microscope. Suddenly, Luna slammed her book shut, the smack of the pages cutting into the silence.

"People talk," she said. She was looking at me but past me, like how my father used to do. Then she paused and focused. "The only real difference between people and animals is that people talk. That's it."

It was the kind of moment that flags itself for you, announces its importance right away but waits till later to be explained. I thought of plenty of reasons to remember the moment right then—how beautiful Luna looked with her face pinched up in thought, how nice it was to know that no matter what anyone said about me and my girlfriend, they couldn't say we weren't smart. But as time passed, what Luna said stayed with me, and soon the question came up: if that's true—if talking makes a person—then what's wrong with me? Why don't I speak?

That's when I started looking for words, I realize now, now that I am still and boxed in quiet, with no one to listen and everything to say. Those words meant the chance to be a person, in my own language, for real.

That moment is as big as a planet for me now. Every day I think about it and find new stars, new rings. I remember it together with our laughter at the pier, just before my world fell from its socket. Now, in the quiet, I remember the seven of us, Luna, LaShanya, TaRonne, Arya, Angelique, Margina, and me—chilling, glowing, taking gulps of the night and sprinkling it out in laughter. I remember our loudness, how huge we felt, in the best way, and how free. I can't say exactly what happened after that, how it started, what the man said, what he did, how we responded. But I remember opening my mouth saying, "*We are people,*" and feeling, believing, that words could help us.

TaRonne

We left the pier with our faces tied tight into smiles, me and my lady in the front. Arya was laughing, her hand all warm and wet in mine. Vernice and Luna were behind us, quiet as usual, cuddled up in each other like West Fourth was their living room. Sha's little friends were holding down the rear, and Sha was on the near side of the curb, brows sharp as switchblades, face in full glow like she was a drag queen walking for femme realness. Before shit went down, the night was nice, cool, everything peace. Then I saw it happen in sepia tone, time winding down to slow motion. I knew shit was wrong before the dude threw his cigarette at us, before he touched Arya's neck, before he slung his threats at Sha. As soon as he called Vernice what he did, I knew there would be a fight.

Me and Arya had had some problems in the car, but she had brought it down to a simmer by the time we got to Sixth Ave. She was finishing up the summer session at Morton Street Middle School, and someone had asked her to make a list of the students that should be kept apart in the future, just so that a gun or a baby didn't show up in class one day. I told her I didn't think that was her place, that by the time they're twelve, kids should be allowed to conduct their little romances and tragedies as they please. She shot me an icicle stare and told me I was naïve. "You can't pretend the teacher's role is strictly intellectual in 2006. Things are not that simple for us, TaRonne." Full first name. I knew she was tight. I told her I knew she wasn't simple, that I liked how complicated she was. She told me "Complex!" and started popping some shit about transitive verbs. I put my arm around her, said I didn't know the difference but was ready to learn. She liked that. By the time we walked past the movie theatre on West 3rd, we were back to our black-dyke-hood-love like in *Set It Off*, all Cleo and Ursula again.

We walked past the newsstand where some skaters and rich kids and a handful of gay boys were scattered around, all talking kiki and enjoying the night. Merengue horns and hip-hop beats hovered over the pavement, and the smells of beer, smoke, and McDonalds's French fries mixed thick on the street. In front of the sex shop on West Third, a homeless woman was sitting on the ground, talking to her scarf, and when we passed the woman, Sha's little richgirl

11

friend stared like she saw an alien, then stepped over the woman like if she wasn't there at all. I whispered in my lady's ear: "Arya, what you think would happen if we brought her back to Newark with us, or took her up to Harlem?"

Arya laughed. "She'd probably front like she wasn't scared, just like she's been fronting all night, trying to be smooth."

I laughed. "I don't know. Maybe it's not a front. Maybe there is some smoothness to her, after all, deep, deep down."

Arya slapped my finger and shot me a look that made me wish we'd stayed in bed that night.

Then I saw him, half a second before he saw us. He looked about thirty-five, although I found out later that he was in his twenties. And from the table he had set up on the pavement, covered with DVDs, I would have sworn he was a bootlegger, although the papers, the prosecutor, and everyone else who mattered called him a "filmmaker" from the next day on. When he opened his mouth at Sha, I didn't care what he called himself.

"Hey, princess!" he said. Sha didn't respond. He didn't give up.

"Sweetheart, I'm talking to you."

"She's not interested," I told him from the far side of the pavement.

"Why don't you let her speak for herself?" He moved from behind the table and took a pull from his cigarette, stretching his neck to see where my voice came from.

"She doesn't have anything to say to you," I said, loud now, getting hot. "She's gay."

Then he looked dead at Verniece, thinking she was the one talking, instead of me.

"Who asked what you think, you goddamn elephant!"

Verniece was shocked frozen, like if someone had snuck up on her and flashed a camera in her face.

"Fuck you, nigga!" I shouted.

"Oh, that was you?" he said, taking another pull and finally turning my way. "You look like a fucking man. What, you sticking up for your woman? Don't go that way, sweetheart." He looked at Sha and grabbed his fly. "I'll fuck you straight!"

I shouted something—I can't remember what, the words and the spit and my teeth all mixed up in my mouth. He flicked his cigarette at us, the cherry arching across space toward Angelique and Margina, who looked like they would piss on theyselves soon, if they hadn't already. We were in motion before the fire landed. I can't really call what happened after that. Wild how time and space make perfect sense up to a point, but then unravel like shoelace threads in the tick of a second. I saw his hand on Sha's neck, in her hair. I felt my fists pushing hard into his shoulder, the blows never landing heavy enough. I saw Angelique and Margina get some hits in too, felt my surprise. I heard some words come from behind me, from Verniece maybe, but I have no idea what they were. I never saw a knife, and I never heard the muthafucka cry. I wish I had.

Arya is the only one who hears me when I say I saw it coming from that one word—elephant—before the spit and the fire and the bodies flew. Everything after that was like dominoes falling into place on a track. Tell my femme friend you want her pussy. Fine. Call me a man. Whatever. None of that is new. But what he had for Verniece was something different, like she wasn't even human. He tore the person out of her, like he tore out that clump of Sha's hair, like the judge tore up our lives and everything we know, chunks of us missing like the truth missing from news stories.

The cops, reporters, lawyer, jury, everyone but my woman skips over that part, that word—elephant—like they want to press fast forward and get to the part of the story that really matters. When the first report came out without mentioning what he called Verniece, Arya said it was because the white reporter didn't see why that kind of "dehumanization" would mean a fight to us. I realized then that Arya is the naïve one. I tried to let that word sit in my ears for a long time after she said it: *dehumanization*. By then I knew I wouldn't get to hear her talk like how she does for a long time. That was our good-bye.

I can't speak for the rest of us, but I was glad when he took that step and put his hands on Sha. Hands you can see, touch, prove. Hands you can bite and burn and tear away. But words, I'm learning, ain't shit.

Sha doesn't know if she stabbed the man. They screamed the question into her face for hours and each time she said "I'm not sure." But I know this—I wish I'da had a knife in my hand, wish I'da heard him shriek like a dying cat under my fingers. I can see that night however I want to see it now, and I see it this way all the time: I'm the one with the knife, and I am sure. This woman sticks it in that nigga real fucking good.

LaShanya

The knife was a gift from my mother. She gave it to me to keep in my purse, because she loves me, because she didn't want me to be the first of the two of us to leave this world. They were killing black dykes in Newark—like they always are, here and everywhere. But now there was Sakia Gunn, my cousin's sister-in-law's friend. Sakia with the deep eyes and the sweet, shy smile, Sakia who was fifteen and could've been me, stabbed to death on the same corner where I used to catch the bus to work, right by the twenty-four-hour police booth, and still nobody saw. Wal-Mart doesn't give time off for hate crime danger, and I had to work late nights all the same. My mother called that knife my bodyguard. She gave it to me to keep me safe. To keep me whole and coming home.

When I think of that night, I think in lists of things. The courtroom is a big wooden box, and as I sit here, my heart tries to fly away from me, but the lists bring comfort, something solid, like place. I think of the smell of my hair grease melting under the streetlights. I think of my newest sisters, Angelique and Margina, wailing behind me as the fire flies at my eyes. I think of the man, the stripes on his shirt getting bigger and bigger until they are on me, right on top. I do not see my knife. I try hard, plunge my fingers into memory. I try to see myself pulling the blade from my bag, try to feel what I have never felt before, my knife slipping past skin, sinking quickslow into flesh. But all I can remember is the weight of his hands on my scalp, those stripes falling on top of me, like how this judge sits on top of the room, hovering like Jesus hovers in holographic paintings on project walls.

Judge McBain, sitting on top of me, his face breaking like a cloud, his cackle crashing over me like lightening. "Sticks and stones may break my bones," he says. He tells us that's what we should have thought. That was the command that should have traveled like blood from our brains to our bodies. Not DUCK, not BLOCK, not PROTECT YOURSELF, YOUR GIRL. As though "I'll fuck you straight" was just a pack of words.

The man has a name, but I'd rather not say it. He's sitting up in the wooden box, just like he sat up in some reporter's face, saying he didn't think it was a crime to "say hello to a human being." I've never felt more alone, more confused than in this moment. I feel like this man and Judge Dickbrain—that is what I want to call him, where they've got me to now—I feel like the two of them come from the same place, someplace where a bootlegger without a pot to piss in and a white man with power dusting his shoulders like dandruff can be two sides of the same damn coin. This is not a place I ever thought I'd be. I did not know I lived there.

But Dickbrain is the bootlegger's parrot in his sentencing speech. "Sticks and stones," he says first. And then: "Words don't justify hurting a human being."

I sit and remember stripes and sounds and hands flying into me like arrows, wonder if either of them knows how good "human being" sounds right now, as a thing to be. Sounds like a safe place in the flow of words and things, something as sure as the ticking of the clock at the back of an old, hollow room. I wonder if either of them will ever know how hard it is to think human, to *be* human, when someone is threatening to knock, force, fuck the *you* out of you.

I hear our names hit like tennis balls across the courtroom and I think: we are women whose names mean things. Luna is bright and distant like the moon she is named for. Verniece is named for her mother, who's more like her than either of them can admit. Arya is named for a beautiful kind of song. Angelique is named for an angel that welcomed her mother to heaven in a dream. Margina is named for her father's choice to forget the center of things and live well on the sidelines. TaRonne is named for a grandmother who spat in a white man's face for calling her "girl," and an aunt who raised all her sisters' children on the salary of a maid. My name comes from Hopi and Spanish and Newark Ghetto, my mother's imagination and a mix of things. I wonder if Judge Dickbrain would have anything to say about that.

But when the thunder quiets and the cloud seals up, what he has to say becomes clear. He forgets about names and drops numbers on us all. Angelique Ramos, Margina Thompson, Arya Lewis: *Six Months Probation*. Luna Martinez: *Three years in prison*. TaRonne Daniels: *Five Years*. Verniece Smith: *Eight Years*. LaShanya Parish: *Ee-leh-ven*.

I will be nineteen tomorrow. The next time I am able to run through a sprinkler on my mother's street, kiss my girlfriend in a quiet room, make myself a turkey sandwich, dance or sing with no one watching, I will be thirty. I will never remember a bloody knife in my hand. No one will ever have to prove it was there.

When we left Verniece's house that night, her mother was on her way to church. While they got the baby dressed, Mrs. Smith asked Verniece over and over to come with her to the service. Verniece said,

"No," sweetly, then strapped on a baby sandal, pulled up a tiny sock. Her mother asked one more time on her way out the door, and Verniece said "No, thank you" again, like she was turning down butter for her toast.

Mrs. Smith held the baby and said to all of us:

"Alright, then. You girls be safe."

We were seven girls to her. Seven women to us. Either way we were people, sure as time.

Verniece

All I do now is remember: I am wrapped up in Luna, my girls, and the warm, licorice sky. The man tears like a bullet through our night.

"Who asked what you think, you goddamn elephant?"

I am afraid for my girls, for Luna, and for myself. I see him reach for Sha, his palms spread wide and ready to grab, and I think of her mother, of my mother, of Anthony Jesús. I don't know what will happen. Then, the thing Luna said wails in my ears: *The only difference between people and animals.* And my own words swirl up into orbit: *You are a person.*

So many things are going on in this moment, I feel like my mind is breaking down to mesh, to screen. I cannot tell what is happening inside, what out. I see a man in pink come, I see a woman run away. I see fingers and DVD cases and a nugget of fire fly. I see Luna and my mother holding the baby, smelling good like ackee and saltfish. I see blood curled around stripes, and Sha holding a silver-soaked blade. From one side of my ears or the other I hear him say again: "Goddamn," "God-damned," "God-dammned elephant." I feel my words popping like firecrackers inside my mouth, and I let them blaze the air:

You are not a man - Your sneakers are cheap your clothes are corny you have no job - You are not a man, hands on your sleepy little dick trying to prove it's there - You are not a man, what you know about God some white man in the sky—If your God doesn't know me blackdykemanwoman god fuck him he's doesn't exist—You are not a man—You are a joke.

All those words, all that time, beat into nothing like bubbles on the wind.

Columns of newspaper ink are burned into my eyes now. I try to make faces out of the lines and curves. I do not want to read what they say about us. I would rather see anything else. In one paper, I see my mother's head turning toward our apartment door, an almost-eclipse of black hair and a crescent of powdered cheek. In another, I see Luna's proud neck, Anthony Jesús's sourdough chin. I say nothing, think less than nothing—just try to pull their faces through the ink.

My first night here, I make a decision: pretend. I play games with myself, pretend to fool myself like my mother used to do when she didn't want to really see me. I tell myself things are not what they are. I pretend that things are me and Luna and the baby, slow-swirling mornings dappled with laughter, endless hours of warmth and clean air. If I want to share my dinner with Anthony Jesús, I decide he's on my lap, his polka-dot bib brushing my wrist. When I miss TaRonne and Sha so much it hurts my chest, I decide they're here on the cot with me, and we laugh.

I wade through the sea of orange suits, eat my food, and do what I'm told. I try not to think in days, how they close me up in darkness, stuff all my holes with funk and pain. I try not to think of how time is crusting over, baking me deeper into stillness each time the moon brings a day to its end. But there is always the ink, running like blood up and down the newsprint paper. Even when I say nothing, the headlines are always there: KILLER LESBIANS' TRIAL BEGINS... SEETHING SAPPHIC SWARM DESCENDS... BLOODTHIRSTY PRIDE ATTACKS.

On the morning after my first night here, someone puts a newspaper in my hands. It's folded open, and before I read the headlines, I find my name in the middle column, a gnarl of ink at the center of the page. "Verniece Smith, 19, was hauled out of the courtroom after an emotional outburst. 'I'm a mother,' Smith wailed." I read up from there, wading back through the spread of letters, grabbing onto the lines and curves I can find sense in. I float up through my girls' names and ages, the number of years each of us will lose starting now. Then I see the headline: LESBIAN WOLFPACK HOWLS ITS END.

This is when I decide to make things whatever I want them to be. If I cannot be a person I decide, then anything can be anything at all. I find Luna's hand in the paper, our baby's eyes in the black of the ink. From the space around me, I carve my mother's smile and a deep, wetwarm sky.

I get up, tighten my grip, and breathe. Then I part my lips, clear my throat, and say—out loud—"*Let's go.*"

Blue Talk and Love

In the halls of Madison Avenue Day School, she was known as tall Xiomara, Xiomara of the wispy bean-sprout hair, of the rubber-band arms and manila folder skin, forever slurping soda through a striped and bending straw. Before she sat on Earnestine's bed, Earnestine watched her as everyone did—through a film of awe and envy—pressing their faces toward her like children fixed to the glass wall of an aquarium, marveling at their majesty of a family of whales, begrudging them the simplicity of the lives they seemed to live.

If Xiomara Padilla was a legume, Earnestine—born Rakisha Earnestine Davis-Sanchez—was the brown, bulbous potato that smart Upper East Side women pushed to the sides of their plates at the start of dinner. Earnestine was big and black and boring. She lived in the Hamilton Heights section of Harlem, in a brownstone the color of plain construction paper. It was the kind of house that looked nice enough from the front, but that would quickly reveal, to anyone who entered, that its walls were peeling in glacial scraps and that its old, tired floors were sinking under their own weight, taking their sweet time in falling apart.

Her parents were unable to do much in terms of upkeep—her mother was a minister and her father was a musician, which meant that her mother's life was busy and her father's was a mystery. Earnestine left the house every morning with her already-blockish body tensed and pinched, her shoulders hunched and her arms fanning out from her middle like the limbs of a frightened camper, ever on the ready to intimidate a bear.

On the first day of sixth grade, Earnestine discovered that she was the color and shape of Oobleck, a lifeless science class concoction made of cornstarch, water, and coffee grounds, used to demonstrate the properties of plasma, to prove that some things were hopelessly sturdy, even if they were liquid inside. She understood Oobleck's place in the chain of elements right away. When Mr. Halstring, the science teacher, asked for a volunteer to sit in the empty seat next to the sunlamp he'd affixed to the tropical milkweed plant the class was to grow that term—"Someone with a tough skin who can take the heat," he said with an awkward smirk—Earnestine was not surprised to find the whole class's eyes on her, including Xiomara, whose desk sat beside the empty chair. And because she was interested in seeing things change—and for that reason alone—Earnestine raised her hand.

Despite their differences, Earnestine and Xiomara did have some things in common. Both were brown-girl cheese-bussers who lived fathoms away from school in the tight crevice between Harlem and Washington Heights. Xiomara and her mother lived next to the Sanchez-Davis home, in a mammoth-sized tenement building that towered over the block's row of five proud but portly brownstones, of which Earnestine's family's was the last. Whenever Earnestine's parents fought about the family's bills or Earnestine's grades or her father's joblessness or anything else, she would steal four cigarettes from her father's coat pocket and creep down to the tiny plot of fenced-in pavement behind the brownstone that passed for a backyard. She would stand on a broken yard chair and call Xiomara's name, pelting her window with plastic hairbeads or sunflower seeds. Eventually, if Xiomara was not out with a boy, or busy on the phone, or painting her toenails, she would come over. Earnestine would lead her quickly through her bedroom and into the small backyard, where the two girls would smoke under the emerald-green weed trees and talk about boys.

Out there in the yard, Earnestine felt that she and Xiomara were alone in a secret tropical cave beneath a post-apocalyptic city sometime around the year 2020—an impossible distance away. The brownstone walls on their side of the street were all dilapidated, their dingy paint falling in chunks like stalagmites, their windows either boarded up like drawbridge doors or gaping open like the mouths of intergalactic portals to unthinkable worlds. On the opposite side of the yard was another huge tenement building, which was covered with neon-colored ivy weeds and overlooked a sprawling lot full of wild trees, overgrown grass, and Technicolor trash. The city's sanitation services did not manage to keep up with Northern Harlem's waste production, and so, with nowhere else to put their trash, people appeared at the windows of the tenement at all hours, smoking weed, declaring love to their mothers, waging complaints about the noisy neighbors down the hall. Always, they dropped something—a cigarette butt, a soda can, a dirty diaper—as if to punctuate their joy or ire. Occasionally, Earnestine would hear a large stairwell window slide open, its metals rubbing like a brandished sword, and a great crash would follow as a broken salon-style hair dryer or an overused sofa fell down on the trash heap.

One warm day a week into the school year, Earnestine managed to coax Xiomora down with less fuss than usual, simply by waving a couple of cigarettes in the air. The girls sat on Myrna Davis's warped yard table, their feet dangling down over the broken chairs. Xiomara leaned back on the table, her weight propped on the pads of her palms, the cigarette poking up between her slim fingers. During a lull in conversation, she stooped to pick a loose hunk of concrete from the ground, tracing its grooves with her nails. Then she looked up, her body loose as a thin-stretched cloud.

"Alex Orwell is kinda fly," she said. Her voice sprayed in cool tones over the pavement like a sprinkler in the summertime. Earnestine sat stiffly beside her, her hands a jumble of brown in her lap. "And anyway he can help me do math, which is dope."

Xiomara leaned her head to the side and let her hair lick at Earnestine's bare arms, arching her eyebrows in Earnestine's direction. Earnestine inched away quickly. She scratched her elbows, made magnets of her knees, and pressed her fingers tighter around her cigarette, trying not to notice the smell of Xiomara's hair—smoke and cherry lip gloss.

"Why you acting like that?" Xiomara said. She rolled her eyes and looked into the trash mound while Earnestine sat frozen in a dumb shrug. "You act like we're at school or something, like you trying to be all proper for your boyfriend, Mr. Halstring." She sighed and blew a funnel of smoke into the air. "I hate how Madison Avenue Day people act. Like if their mommies are there all the time, hiding in their pocket, about to jump out and smack them if they do anything too loud or too close. So *immature*."

She closed her eyes, her verdict delivered, and swayed her small, round head to the sound of a song Earnestine could not hear, and Earnestine knew she was gone.

When this happened, which it almost always did, Earnestine felt like the last person left alone in a movie theater, traces of sound and scent the only evidence that she had ever been anything but alone. If Xiomara was not too bored or too busy to stay, they would continue to smoke until the cigarettes were done, then throw the butts over the gaping fence into the trash-filled lot. But if Xiomara left, which she did often, abruptly, and without explanation, Earnestine would put the cigarettes out on the bottom of her sneaker and lodge the stubs under one of the loose concrete slabs, saving them in case of some future emergency, which only she seemed to believe might ever come.

Xiomara was indefatigably bright. All the white people at Madison Avenue Day counted her resilience among her many charms. Her father was a young Dominican immigrant, like Earnestine's, but unlike Ernesto Sanchez, Fernando Padilla had died in a drug-related gunfight on the block back in the eighties, when the girls were six. Xiomara's mother was a thin white woman from New Jersey whose hollow-cheeked face reminded Earnestine of a Halloween ghost mask, and who was always at the City Municipal Services building, where she worked as a clerk. When she did come home, she went straight into the kitchen to drink amaretto sours until she was dancing cheek-to-cheek with the plastic folding table. But somehow, by all indications, Xiomara did more than alright for herself. Her elastic smile and unwavering ease seemed to win her most of what she wanted—the choice spot in science class from Mr. Halstring, homework help from the Madison Avenue Day boys, a solid half of Earnestine's stolen cigarettes.

While Xiomara talked about her many admirers, Earnestine listened, chimed in when she could, and pretended to be more interested than she was. In truth, Earnestine liked boys like she liked anybody else. If they were nice to her or had round, symmetrical features, she liked them. If they were very funny or very sad, she liked them. If they gave her cigarettes or invited her over to drink from their parents' wine cellars, as did James Schaffran, the eighth grade Goth whose every word rode the loose end of a sigh, Earnestine liked them. Yet the real excitement in talking about boys with Xiomara was not in the thought of the boys themselves, but in the way the talking made her feel. In those conversations, Earnestine became different versions of herself, like a paper doll putting on a newly-traced and cut out dress for each fantasy. When she kindled up a crush on Perry Stoltz, a sporty boy with hair the color of burnt toast, she imagined herself as a light-skinned black

Barbie, her face the shape of an almond and her body long and sleek like Xiomara's hair. When her attentions turned to Owen McDonough, a loud-mouthed alterna-geek, she saw herself as a punk rocker, with fruit punch-red braids and a waist that curved in like the slope of an electric guitar. Xiomara, of course, did not need to stretch her imagination so far. While Earnestine prattled on about the dreams she'd had about Perry or Owen or So-and-So, Xiomara talked about the homework they'd done for her, the notes they'd passed to her, how their teeth tasted under her tongue. "They're *aight*, or whatever," she would say between pulls, looking off into the trash heap. "But in the end they're like Pop Tarts. They're OK at first, but pretty soon you see they're kinda wack, actually. They're never what you want—they're just what's around."

But for Earnestine, even such disappointment seemed a luxury. And so she should have hated Xiomara. And if you caught her on a bad day, she would have said she did hate her—deeply and with a full-heartedness not unlike glee. This is what she said to Jacob Morton, a screw-faced boy with the fancy calculator, who accosted her with the question one afternoon in September, three days before Xiomara sat on her bed.

"Why does Xiomara hang out with you?" he shouted at her, swooping down into her face like a bat as she finished her Social Studies homework. "She doesn't even like you. She told Samantha Fitzpatrick that she hates you. She thinks you have B.O."

"Good," Earnestine said plainly, taking care not to look up from her text book. She turned the page as

27

casually as she could. "'Cause I hate her, and I *know* she has B.O."

"You're just jealous because you look like a guy," he said, opening his backpack and producing a pack of coveted Sour Power candies. He piled the sparkling gummy strings into his mouth and continued talking, his teeth gleaming with green slime. "What you should do," he said, "is stop wearing those stupid dresses and just pretend you're a guy. Then you can be her boyfriend."

Earnestine felt heat at her ears. It was a familiar line of insult, but this had a new sting. She knew what Madison Avenue Day School thought of her, but no one had ever dealt her the blow of comparing her to Xiomara. It felt unfair, below the belt, even for sixth graders. Earnestine opened her mouth in hopes that a brilliant rebuttal would come out, but there was nothing. So she reached up, grabbed the Sour Powers from Jacob, and hustled to her feet as quickly as she could. She poured all of the gummy cords in her mouth at once and hurled the crumpled paper bag hard at his face. Then she turned, doing her best to keep her spine straight, keep her eyes forward, to let him see nothing but her back as she shuffled away.

She tried to erase that encounter from her mind, but Jacob Morton's words stayed with her from that afternoon through the agonizing first weeks of the school year. Jacob had exposed a terrible fact: Earnestine's clothes were stupid, it was true. Her mother had begun to read up on African religious syncretisms just before Earnestine started fifth grade, and had decided to dress the entire family in homemade African-inspired getups from that point on.

Earnestine liked the fabrics her mother used—their colors and geometiric patterns reminded her of Easter eggs and outer space at once. But the shapes of the clothes themselves were awful. Skirts as round as basketballs, pants whose legs clung in anguish to her calves, and whose low crotches swung wildly between her thighs like a cow's udders. Earnestine liked the idea of Africa well enough. She listened happily to her parents' stories about Marcus Garvey and Liberian settlement, dreaming of the things she might change when her own life began. Still, things had their times and their places, she felt, and lunchtime in the minty halls of Madison Avenue Day School was neither the time nor the place for a Back-to-Africa movement. Earnestine already felt as big and black as a Dark Continent. Kente crowns and cowrie shells were the last things she needed.

Xiomara did not have this problem—before the bed or ever. She sailed into school every day like a lucky feather waiting to be caught and wished on. After Earnestine stole Jacob's Sour Powers, Xiomara floated up beside him smiling, whispered something in his ear, and drifted away with the remainder of his allowance in her pocket. Her smile was like Alice's pack of magical sweetcakes, growing and shrinking her haphazardly, though always to positive effect. The "eat me" smile Xiomara launched at Jacob was as wide as a bowl of milk, and it made her body seem to stretch so high upward that she could grab a chunk of sun and smear it on her cheeks like blush. But then, to the Madison Avenue Country teachers, she gave a demure smile as tight and quiet as a yellow raisin, reducing herself down to an unfinished hope, a glimmer of pale brown potential. They liked that.

So if you asked Earnestine on a bad day what she really thought of Xiomara, she would have drawn her eyebrows up into her hairline, rolled her neck halfway around its orbit and said "I hate that ho." And she may nearly have convinced you, not because it was true, but because Earnestine's bad days were very bad. On days when she was bleeding, or when she left the house too late to stuff her bag with cookies while her mother wasn't watching, Earnestine had nothing but shrill looks and sour words for anyone. And when her parents' arguments kept her up into the slim hours of the morning, Earnestine spent all of the following day in what her mother would call a "funk," her face set in a pit-bull glare from the first sirens of the morning until the streetlight came on at night.

Her least favorite day was Sunday, when she would usually be forced to go to her mother's church or to spend the day feigning sickness, the only acceptable excuse for missing the service. It was on Sunday mornings that she began to dread the start of the week, which meant facing not only Madison Avenue Country but also ARYSE—short for African Rites for Young Sisters' Empowerment—the rites-of-passage program that she had to attend every Monday in order to have her own big coming-of-age party and not miss out on all her classmates' Bat Mitzvah fun. Earnestine hated ARYSE, not only because she resented having to learn about housekeeping and feminine hygiene along with black history and financial planning, but also because ARYSE was filled with girls like Xiomara and worse. These girls were all prettier than Earnestine could ever hope to be, and yet, unlike Xiomara, they were like her—black girls with black mothers who worked to give them everything they themselves hadn't had coming up—including pride in their roots—and with fathers who were, in some fashion, gone. Her failure to fit in with these girls could not be attributed to her blackness or her mother's taste or anything other than the endless vacuum of space and synapse that was simply Earnestine. At Madison Avenue Day, Earnestine was an anomaly. At ARYSE she was a mistake.

On the day Xiomara sat on her bed, Earnestine woke up into a familiar pit of Sunday dread, pained to see the weekend thin away, horrified at the thought of facing Madison Avenue people *and* the ARYSE girls the following day. She was greeted into the morning by the sound of her parents fighting upstairs, which added to her distress. She lingered in bed for a few minutes, pulling the covers up to her chin and imagining herself sinking deep into the fibers of the mattress. Then she got up, crept to the kitchen to pour herself a small mixing-bowl full of Cocoa Krispies, and she set herself up in the living room where she could put on *Saved By the Bell* and listen to the argument from under the blue-and-white flicker of the television.

"I'm all for exposing her to African culture," her father said. "But tell me why I have to be there when all those women swoop in to take their little Nubian princess chickadees home. You never been there as me, Myrna. You don't know how it feels. I'm tired of being the only one. Don't you get that?" The floor sighed. "*Diablo.*"

"She's not even thirteen yet, Ernesto," her mother said. "We can't have her walking the city alone at

night. This isn't the safe little place you want it to be."
Her many bracelets chimed. "I'm sorry."

Spoon in hand, tongue adrift in chocolate mush,
Earnestine sympathized with her father. It was true
that he was the only father ever to come to ARYSE,
and the ARYSE mothers always made a big deal of
him. They seemed to Earnestine to morph into
overgrown cartoon witches around him, toting pans of
bread pudding and candied yams, their faces all grin
and batted lash as they explained that they'd just made
too much food for their own little families of two. But
Myrna Davis had to work, she told Ernesto, and it was
selfish for him to complain about picking Earnestine
up when she was the one who put food on the table
and paid Madison Avenue Day's tuition while he sat
around doing God Knew What and playing his music,
which, Earnestine knew, everyone in the family loved
more than they'd say.

"And you haven't played a gig in months," her
mother added. "What do you do up there all day,
anyway? Will I ever get to know?" But Ernesto gave
no reply.

Earnestine closed her ears to this part of the
conversation. She tried not to think about how her
father spent his days, fearing small betrayals even
more than large ones. A dead body, a secret family,
even a sex change would have been easy enough to
manage, Earnestine thought. Her parents would
divorce, the house would be sold, and she would begin
a new life as a new girl elsewhere. But subtler
insurgencies made her feel jittery. It was the small,
hidden questions of her parents' lives that scared her—
whether they picked their noses in secret, how long

each sat sighing on his or her side of the bed before pulling on their shoes in the morning. How lonely each really was. Her biggest fear was that her father's secrets were not mean, not cruel, but sad.

When the TV show was over, Earnestine dumped the cereal bowl in the kitchen sink and plodded back to her room where she waited for her father's music to spring up as it always did after a fight. Ernesto was a brilliant musician, though not a particularly talented artist. His gift was not in creating great expressions of feeling, but in recasting familiar songs so that their meanings transformed. He turned Michael Jackson's "Can't Help It" into a blues-filled dirge, while Donnie Hathaway's "A Song for You" became a raucous church hymn in his hands. Earnestine knew that this fight would end as most of her parents' fights did, with slammed doors, unfinished sentences, and her father's steady baritone lacing someone else's words through the brownstone's hallways, tying the loose ends as best it could.

Soon she heard her mother leave, tossing a weary "good-bye" behind her. Then she heard her father's keyboard as always, though this time, the notes sounded closer than usual. He was playing Earth, Wind and Fire's "September," one of her mother's favorite songs. Earnestine sat on her bed and listened. She had heard the song many times before—she even thought she could remember seeing her parents dance to it once or twice in the kitchen while her father cooked dinner, her father whisking her mother into his arms and swirling her around the counter, a greasy spatula glistening in his free hand while he sang to her mother from her favorite line: "only blue talk and love, remember?" Earnestine liked the song well enough, though she did not know if the memory could be trusted. The original version was quick and catchy, and carried with it a breathlessness that did remind Earnestine of the month of September, the smell of freshly-Cloroxed school lockers and crisp erasers, the quiet pain of a blank year sprawling ahead. But her father's "September" today was different. It was a ballad, a relentless tale of loss that brought to mind all of the things she feared most about love, and made her wonder how people managed to grow up at all.

The music paused as Earnestine made her way up to the first floor, eager to grab the cigarettes and go smoke in the sparkle of the weeds and waste. Stopping at the coat rack, she peered around the corners to be sure her father was not around. She fished through his pocket for the smokes, but found nothing but gum wrappers, paper clips, pennies, and dimes. Disappointed, she gathered the change and headed back down to the garden floor, planning to salvage a stub from her concrete stash. But when she reached the bottom of the stairs, she found the yard door open and her slab upturned. Her father's keyboard sat on the table, its white keys flickering gray under the shade of the weed trees. Ernesto sat on one of the two unbroken chairs, his back toward her, a large Cerveza Presidente open on the table. A cigarette dangled from his lips like an old-school soothsayer's chew stick.

Earnestine lingered in the doorway, wondering if he had heard her, or if she still had time to disappear. Just as she resolved to make a run for it, he spoke.

"*Que tu 'ta buscando, mija*?" he said. "You looking for me?"

She stuffed the change into her pocket as quietly as she could and moved closer.

"No," she said. "Just wanted some air."

He turned toward her and pulled out the other working chair, motioning for her to join him. His face was flat and still. Had she not heard him play just seconds before, she would have thought he had been sitting there in quiet contemplation for hours.

"What is it about this sister-passage thing anyway?" he said, his eyes warm and glassy. "Do they really tell you anything your mama and I don't tell you? Anything you need to know?"

She paused. The smell of fresh biscuits whipped into the air from a neighboring building, laying a thin, sweet film over the garbage-thick air.

"Not really," she said. "I hate it. School too."

Ernesto nodded, his eyes tracing the jagged picket fence that circled the yard, the missing planks of which gave it the worn but hopeful look of a six-year-old's smile.

"The girls," he said slowly. "Right? The pretty ones."

Earnestine didn't answer.

"*Amor mío*," he said, his voice heavy with smoke and tenderness. "Fine—those girls are *lindas*, with their long hair and their boyfriends. But you have something they will never have, whatever they do. You have pain. *Duende*. Your mama calls it soul."

Earnestine considered the words, rolling them around in her mouth as she had seen her mother do with red wine at restaurants downtown. Soul seemed simple, something everyone had, though few knew how to work it. But *duende* was new. The word curved around itself softly, took its own brief but mysterious dips and turns. She reached for the pack of Marlboros on the table, eyeing her father for a response, and held a cigarette to her lips. Ernesto turned his head and looked into the next yard, where a pair of pigeons had begun to peck at each other's necks. Slowly, he slid the matchbook toward her with an ashy elbow.

Earnestine lit the cigarette and held it in the air as casually as she could, her wrist bent like a bird of paradise flower, the way Xiomara did sometimes. When she inhaled too deeply and started to cough, Ernesto whipped his face back toward her, slid the beer across the table. She sipped only enough to clear her throat, then pushed the bottle back.

"*Mira esos pájaros*," Ernesto said, turning away again. "They're not *swans* or *doves*, or fuckin *nightningales*. They're pigeons. They're gray and they waddle and they all have *tetas grandotas*, even the male ones. It could be embarrassing, what people might say about them. They go through shit. They get little snot-nosed children running after them, shooting them with their pissy water guns. But *míralos*," he said, his back still toward her. "They got their own thing. Let shit go down, let the world end, man, and it's them, and the rats, and the roaches gonna take over. They're not even worried about humans. They do what they feel."

Earnestine took another pull and watched her father's neck sway like a string beneath a helium balloon. Then she watched the pigeons, their bulging grey breasts flashing diamonds of muted purple and turquoise as they necked. She inhaled the smoke, the trash, the beer, the baking bread, the mild coconut smell of her father's hair grease and the smell of urine that had sprung up from a yard nearby. She watched her father watch the pigeons, sure now of how alone he seemed, perhaps always.

Earnestine opened her mouth to say something—she wasn't sure what—but Ernesto turned toward her before she got a sound out. He eased the cigarette from her hand and dropped it in the pit, then slid the loose slab of concrete back into place.

"Take a shower, mija, before your mama comes home," he said. "And brush your teeth," he added. "Twice."

He rubbed his hands on his knees and settled in before his keyboard, pulling its knobby microphone up toward his face and clearing his throat to sing again.

"Only blue talk and love, remember..?"

In the bathroom, Earnestine pulled her T-shirt over her head and turned on the shower faucet. She looked at her parents' toiletries—her father's shaving cream, her mother's Benin musk body oil, her father's razors, her mother's wooden hair pick—each sitting mute and idle on opposite sides of the tub. She imagined Xiomara's bathroom, a carnival of glossy bottles and tubes, Aqua Net and L.A. Looks hair gel nestled among the kinds of thin, fragile combs that always broke in Earnestine's hair. On the commercials and packages for these products, women were always gusting combs through their hair, misting themselves with clouds of hairspray, running and laughing and smiling at men. When the women weren't white, they looked like Xiomara: always light, always thin, with the kind of long, swirling hair Earnestine would never have. Whenever she tried to imagine other women—women like the ARYSE mothers, or her mother, or herself—frozen in scenes of carefree joy like the women on the bottles, she never could. Standing in the bathroom now, she wondered what her father thought of those women, so unlike her and her mother, women who always seemed nothing but free. She thought of those women and wondered once again what her father did up in that room where she and her mother did not go, how he spent all those hours alone, with no one to share his smokes and his thoughts.

The smell of cheap fried chicken seeped thick through the windows as Earnestine shuffled up to the third floor. She pressed on the studio door and the wood-paneled room opened before her like a broken pumpernickel loaf, its grains lit under the shafts of sun that snuck in from beneath the curtains. She eyed the space—the gleaming drum and cymbal set, the broken keyboards, the empty bottles and guitar picks, the petrified rinds of limes. Settling herself into her father's chair, she swiveled around. The thick edge of a VHS tape stuck out of the TV-VCR console, and when she popped it in, a thin blonde woman sprang to the screen. The woman rode a bicycle down an empty street, her hair flapping behind her like a pile of turning leaves. After a few seconds, the scene changed, and Earnestine was looking at a naked man with faded black socks who sat on a sofa, rubbing at the space between his knees. Soon a doorbell rang on the screen, and the bicycle woman reappeared. She smiled, kissed the man, and began to peel her clothes off in layers, flinging them into the air as though she were throwing confetti.

Earnestine felt queasy at first, but she watched anyway, the smell of hot grease hovering over her skin. She watched the couple's kisses grow slower and longer. Soon, the woman was bent over in front of the man, whipping her hair and shouting to him over her shoulder as the camera flashed close-ups of their sweating skin. Earnestine felt a quiet pang of terror, the same feeling she felt when she stole her father's cigarettes, though this feeling was more bewildering and more intense. She fumbled for the remote and pressed mute. As the camera flashed and zoomed on parts and bodies, Earnestine was not always sure exactly what she was looking at, but she didn't turn it off. Soon the scene changed again. Now the woman sat naked on a sofa, fanning herself with a magazine and smoking a cigarette. Earnestine watched the woman's hair flop against her shoulders to the rhythm of the fan. Every few seconds, the woman peered at the camera with a faint smirk, as though she did not really believe anyone would actually be watching. The woman looked bored and smart and somehow lonely, even as she gave the camera a distant wink. And this made Earnestine think of Xiomara.

Her father's song was still playing when Xiomara came over that afternoon. This time, Earnestine did not lead her out to the backyard. Instead, she sat on the bed and asked her to tell her stories from there.

At first, Xiomara frowned and sucked her teeth. "What's wrong with you?" she said. "Don't you wanna go smoke?"

"No, I mean, I guess, not really," Earnestine stammered, pushing herself back on the mattress. "Maybe we could just hang out here for a minute."

"Oh," Xiomara said, rolling her eyes and landing on the bed in a flop. She smelled like bubble gum and sweat. "So what do you want to do?" She looked at her nails, which were painted a shiny blue.

"I don't know," Earnestine said. "Did you talk to any guys today?"

"Of course," Xiomara said. She rolled her eyes again, but more softly this time, almost generously. She looked at her hands for what felt like a long time, then gathered her hair on top of her head, and looked at Earnestine. Perched on the bed with her arms in the air, her hair a bouquet above her face, Xiomara looked younger and softer and somehow rounder than Earnestine had seen her look before. The expression on her face, too, was different from any other Earnestine had seen there. She looked more unsure, more awake, and less bored.

"So you mean you wanna, like, hang out, in here or whatever?" Xiomara said, her hand still gripping her hair.

Earnestine nodded, willing herself not to inch away. "Yeah," she said. Then she added, "I mean, if you want to."

"But you're not gonna, like, freak out and get all jumpy right?" Xiomara said. "I mean if we, like, talk in here instead?"

Earnestine shook her head. "No," she said. "I don't think so."

She moved a little closer and Xiomara let go of her hair, the waves of it falling over both their shoulders. Xiomara dropped her hands between them on the mattress, and Earnestine put a hand on top of hers, the cool of Xiomara's skin a surprise under

Earnestine's palm, her painted nails smooth under Earnestine's fingers.

"So, I mean, what guys did you talk to?" Earnestine asked. "What did you say to them?"

Beginning a story about a boy she did not bother to name, Xiomara told a tale Earnestine could not believe, about how the boy had promised to buy her a car and to take her to Santo Domingo, where thirteen-year-olds could drive. Their hands still touching, Xiomara told her how the boy's family had offered to find her mother a good job there, how whenever they visited her mother would drink no rum or amaretto—only water and strawberry milkshakes. They took turns inching closer, first Xiomara, then Earnestine, until their arms and faces were touching, too.

"We're moving there soon," Xiomara said, passing her nose along Earnestine's neck. "I'm going to dance *bachata* with my cousins in the mountains. It's my favorite dance. You feel like you're in water when you do it. It can be slow or it can be fast, but either way, you always feel free."

Still talking, Xiomara ran her lips along Earnestine's chin. Earnestine felt her chest jump, then pause, then slow, and she wondered if she should say something, too. But the story continued, and, after a while, she was not sure if it was her voice she heard or Xiomara's, her skin, her hands, her tongue or Xiomara's, whose lips, whose eyes. Pressed together, they shared the hair, trash falling through the sky beyond the back window. The length, and the leanness, and the longing were theirs as her father's song poured its sad notes through the halls.

Snow Fight

This old white nigga starts talking and everybody on the train shuts up real tight for a second. Then they start screaming, *"Eeeeeh! Eeeeeeh!"* cheering like on the basketball court watching Pito and Slimminy try to murder each other one-on-one, or when Sonjra and Ana-Rosario skipped Mr. Dominic's math class to go snatch clothes from on two-fifth and rocked their new Baby Phat jeans straight through eighth period, still with the plastic lock tags on. They ain't even hear what he said, and I'm not gonna front—I didn't really hear it either, it was so loud. I was just surprised to see him put down his newspaper and open his mouth, and even more surprised to see the snow fall out.

And when he said *"Shit!"* forget it—it was a wrap. I always wondered what one of those random old white niggas on the train would do if you touched them or winked at them, rubbed your ass up on them one time when it was crowded or something. I thought maybe they would turn pink and start sweating and pull on they necktie like that old video for "Baby Got Back"—Sir Mix-a-Lot, I think—when the white dude sees the black girl with the phatty and it hits him too close, closer than white people like to go.

But your boy didn't do any of that. All he did was clear his throat and say "HEY!" real loud, like Principal Scaprioni does at assemblies when Light-skin Chris and them is actin' up, singing R. Kelley songs to the girls in the back row. At school, Scaprioni screams "HEY!" louder and they sing louder, going from the Chocolate Factory album and "Step in the Name of Love" straight back to some shit—I can't even remember the title—'bout *"your booody's caaallin fooor me."* Scaprioni says *"HEY"* real loud—not loud as five or ten niggas singin' to cute girls—but who got the microphone? You can feel his voice shaking the walls from out the speakers; if you not talking you can even feel it under your feet.

Me, I sit with my homegirl Patricia and she teaches me words in Spanish. When Chris and them act up she tells me they acting mad *"bobo,"* and when Scaprioni starts sweating like the white dude in the video, his fat face shining like a ham hock, she says *"Que parece cerdo."* I laugh, 'cause my homegirl is funny, and 'cause I like how things she say in Spanish be so close to what I think in English. I don't know, shit like that is just funny to me.

Sometimes, if Dominique showed up to school that day and decided to sit with us instead of her flavor-of-the-week nigga, she bite on her braids like how she do and say some Jamaican shit 'bout *"Dat de man a puar wharff daawg!"* But I'm not good at understanding all that. She make me laugh in the same way, though, for the simple fact that when me and Patricia went to her house, she had oxtails and fried fish with hush puppies, but her whole family called it "oxtail" with no *s*, and "festival." And when Patricia

43

asked what kind of fish it was, Dominique said it was salt fish, but Patricia said she coulda swore it was *bacalao*. Crazy how shit could be different as night and day, then turn out to be the same damn thing just in a different language or a different sauce. I don't know, I just laugh.

Principal Scaprioni doesn't usually have to shake the ground more than once, even though they say 155 is the worst school in the city. They only say that because them dumb-ass twins Andrew and Alex put on some black T-shirts and brought heat to school last year—their senior year, okay, in *April*, not even two months before their graduation—and tried to shoot the nose off the sphinx statue in the lobby, talking 'bout "THIS IS POLITICAL!" Now we have to go through metal detectors every time we come in and out. The line be down the street, almost to the train station. And still they expect us to get to class on time. What is that? And now we 'posed to be these bad-ass kids, meanwhile the worst shit that happens on a regular day is some dumb-ass, bobo-ass, wharff daawg-ass niggas singing "Sex Me!" to a bunch of eighth grade girls who can't even be bothered.

Well, I guess that's not true, depending on how you look at it. What shit does go down at 155 is 'cause they send these teachers whose names are probably Mary-Jane and Becky-Sue to come teach us—like thirty-five heads if everybody would show up—offa three or four books and a halfa piece of chalk. Even when niggas do have the book, half of them can't read for shit 'cause they didn't have the book last year, or any year before that. So what are they gonna do? Act up. I feel bad for the Mary-Janes sometimes.

September they be really trying, lazy blonde hair all combed up, button down shirts and everything. They come in with all these books they photocopied and name tags they make in crayon to show us they really want to learn our names. By June they be done got attitude from the whole class, cursed the class themselves, then cried, and cried some more. Or if not they just broke out before they had the chance. But then I think harder and don't feel sorry for them at all. They go home to Long Island, the Hamptons or some shit. I go home to 143rd.

The Mary-Janes don't know what to do with us, but Scaprioni knows how to shut niggas up. On the news and in the movies they front like principals are some bitch-ass dudes who just love the kids so much they can't find it in they hearts to control them. Picture that. Scaprioni is not scared of a damn body. He is quick to throw you out of the auditorium, or your classroom, or his office, or wherever, and send you right down to the glass box in the lobby with the security guard. (There's two, and people say they both Five-O. I don't know 'bout all that, but I know they have heat and that's all I really need to know.)

If it's the white security guard, you're lucky. He just makes you sit in the box with your eyes closed so you can't make faces to any of your peoples that might pass by. But if it's the black dude, it's a wrap for you. He'll sit you with your back to the door, shove a book under your face, and tell you you better not touch it for any reason other than to turn the page. He hem niggas up with books like *They Came Before Columbus,* about black people been in America earlier than the pilgrims, or *Cultura Afrocaribeña,* about Dominicans

45

and Puerto Ricans really came from Africa and just try to front. One time Dominique got caught messing with some Haitian nigga in the bathroom, and when the teachers found them they got sent straight to the box (nobody even called Scaprioni). Well, it was the black guard, and he sewed them both up tight. She had to read a book about *When Chickenheads Come Home to Roost*, and the Haitian dude got stuffed up with *The Life of Toussaint L'Ouverture.*

That nigga does not play for real. You will be stuck up in that box with nuthin' to look at but either some long-ass book or the shot-up sphinx statue, which still has its white people nose on 'cause Alex and Andrew couldn't aim for shit and shot a hole in the left paw instead. Between the book and the sphinx, you might as well look at that book. And the black guard, if he even catches you with your eyes above page level for a few seconds, he will keep you there in that glass box till the building closes. And that's not till seven thirty, after everyone on the playground *been* took it to the train, so you woulda missed mad shit, like today with the old white nigga.

I'ma be real with you. I actually like staying late at school. If it's warm, we have a really nice time. Niggas play ball, shirts and skins. Females watch and try to look all cute. It's like a fashion show— *America's Next Top Hood Model* and shit—for the ones that have money like that. And even the ones that don't, we can watch. After school it's everybody together, and there's too many of us for Scaprioni and the Mary-Janes to do a damn thing about us, really— other than try to make us leave.

When it's warm, not like now, niggas be runnin'

around the courtyard and dancing crazy. Dominique and Patricia and me maybe start a game of double-dutch, and sometimes even some of the ninth grade girls will jump in. Then we sing all our playground songs from back in the P.S. days, back when we thought cursing was some hot shit: "*1,2, my boyfriend wants to do me, 2,3, he wants to fuck my coochie...*" We sing loud 'cause we can, and we say whatever we want 'cause it be so loud that nobody can hear us.

The best part of staying late at school is when it's warm and you chill outside you can just listen to people speak their languages. It gets so uncomfortable having to talk to the Mary-Janes and Becky-Sues all day, for those of us who try. Talking like you're reading from a book or some shit, like wearing a turtleneck sweater, how it stuffs up your throat. After school on the courtyard, none'a that. Niggas talk like how they fuckin' talk: "This bitch" this and "yo, son" that. The Haitians talk their African-French that is so pretty, and the Jamaican girls go on and on so fast I have to get Dominique to whisper to me just so I can know what's going on.

But in the wintertime, like now, it's different. Only the straight-up *bobo*s and *wharff daawg*s stand around the playground, smoking cigarettes. Everybody else takes it to the train. That's when me and Patricia say bye, 'cause she lives on the A and I take the 1-9. Dominique and me, we do us, though. We sit close as we can get to the middle of the train and listen to the Washington Heights niggas fill up the whole seven cars with loud-ass Spanish: "*Eres preciosa, amor, es un placer...*" This scraggly-looking Dominican nigga is trying to spit game to a light-skinned girl. "*¿Nena,*

Eres freshman?" She don't seem to know how to respond, I guess she too young.

Down at the other end of the car they are talking so loud I can't hear a damn thing, they laughing and running their mouths 'bout *"¡Diablo, que'esa vaina!"* I don't know exactly what they're saying, but it's loud as hell, and it sounds like they having a good time. Dominique is too, talking to some dude I have never seen, so I just sit quietly and do me, try to pick more words out the air.

Then I notice this old white nigga, his back all bent over like a pterodactyl or some shit, this *Jurassic Park* nigga, face all up in a newspaper. He's not making no noise, but his lips are moving fast as the keys on one of those old-ass typewriters from the movies, and I am wondering how long he's gonna ignore all this noise bumping up against him.

When the doors open at 125th, the only outside stop on this side of the city, Light-skin Chris jumps out the door, and I think that's weird 'cause he lives on my block and we both get off at 145th. But then he comes back into the train with a handful of snow and throws it cross the whole car and hits Slimminy right on his neck. Everybody is like *"Ooooh!"* and niggas start laughing. The train makes that doorbell noise to let you know the doors are about to close, but Slimminy sticks his little foot between them and reaches out. The doors click and bang against his foot like they don't know what to do, till then he comes back in with a whole armful of snow. Now it's on. Everybody's laughing and cheering in no language at all, really. Some girls in the middle of the car reach out there, too, and start flicking snow at each other. The bells keep ringing and niggas keep blocking the doors, reaching out and throwing big-ass handfuls of dirty snow at each other.

Then I catch it. And I'm glad right then that I am the kind of person that watches shit instead of getting caught up in it. Light-skin Chris was aiming for Slimminy, but his right hand slipped down the pole he was leaning on. He lost his balance, and the old white nigga got caught in the face with a clump of nasty, dirty, gray snow. Chris looked like he saw his mama ghost coming for him.

"HEY!" the old white nigga goes, like Principal Scaprioni, and everyone shuts up quick, like if he was gonna send them to the glass box or expel them. Then, I don't know, everybody starts cheering, screaming eight times louder than before, like if the Knicks would win a championship—like that. Like this was the best, funniest shit in the world. This old white nigga, the only one on the train fulla mad rowdy, laughing *us*, and he gets caught in the face with dirty snow, and what was he gonna do? Niggas cracking up.

Then he says something: "something-something, *SHIT!*" And it's over. People is dying, laughing so hard. Dominique is biting her braids hard now, looking like she 'bout to piss herself. The door bells ring again and nobody stops them this time, everybody caught up in laughing so hard. Then the snow falls out old boy's mouth and niggas laugh some more. They keep laughing after that and then they go back to doing their thing, just a little more loud and a little more happy.

But you know, I watched. And I'm glad too. 'Cause with everything that went down, the funniest shit to me—the part of this story that nobody else even knows—is the way your boy tried so hard to keep his typewriter lips straight while everybody was laughing. It was me, just me. I'm the only one that caught this old white nigga stretching his face over his teeth and scrunching up his neck and his eyes just to keep from laughing with us. I never woulda guessed that after all that, even this old white nigga himself would have an urge to smile. I don't know, shit like that is just funny to me.

Powder and Smoke

Eyes closed, Saleema fell through the doorway carelessly, blissfully, and landed on the dormitory bed as though there were no doubt in her mind that it was there and ready to catch her. She raised her hands over her head and *smiled in*, as she had always called it, relaxing her muscles and reveling in the warmth of her own face until she felt something like a grin peek at her from inside. She smelled that girl's cigarette smoke in her braids, around her eyes, on her skin. This day was going to be good. Most mornings, Saleema woke up angry at the day—at its rush of classes and its papery post-seminar chatter in these strange Berkshire mountains. She often felt like the largest, darkest, most salient of all the things around her—including the mountains themselves—and the strangest in many ways. For most of her time there, all she had wanted to do those mornings was leave. But now, a semester into her freshmen year, there was *that girl*—the black girl, the city girl, the gum-popping girl from Brooklyn, come as a transfer student to live down the hall. And finally, after weeks of hoping and fretting, of becoming close friends—real friends—Saleema had spent the afternoon with her—and then the evening and the night—smoking

51

Newports and reading Alice Walker while the Biggie Smalls played on the stereo. They hadn't touched and they hadn't needed to; today, the spending time was enough. Now, Saleema felt high and unconquerable like some unnamed constellation. She found herself welcoming the morning. She was thankful for the day and for the fact that she was there. It didn't matter that she still wasn't sure where "there" was, exactly.

Before last night, Saleema had not been a fan of too much quiet or too much sun. So she had left the shade down and the TV on as she usually did lately, set to the talk-show rerun channel she and her homegirls used to watch at home. The TV had played all night while she was gone, and now, as she lay on the bed, the flicker of the small screen lit the space sporadically, revealing in flashes her piles: mail from home, mail from school, bills to pay (these wedged, unopened, behind the garbage can). There were old issues of *The Source* and *Hip-Hop! Magazine*, Lane Bryant and 16 Plus shopping bags, diet columns clipped from magazines and sent by her mother, low-fat cracker boxes, ashy with crumbs. But Saleema ignored all this. Instead, she let herself notice only the things that could feed the greedy joy that girl had inspired. Hands in her hair and reaching only with her skin, Saleema felt the home-things: the letters from her homegirls pinned to her corkboard, written in splotchy ink from dollar-store pens; the Jay-Z poster on her closet door; the rusted "Welcome to Harlem" street sign, ripped off the 145th Street bridge and sent up here to the ivy-crusted boonies by her oldest friend back home.

Now the television blared familiar commercials: "Sealy PosturePedic, Serta Perfect Sleeper, and Simmons Beauty Rest... even lower than the leading quality flatbeds."

"Dial one-eight hundred M-A-T-T-R-E-S," she belted without regard for key or tune, "And leave off the last *S* for Savings!"

She laughed and sang the song again with the soul of Aretha and the deliberate style of Ella. Then she sat up. It was a new feeling, and a delicious one: she wanted to *go*, as usual, but today it almost didn't matter where.

"We haven't seen you, Saleema!"

"Yeah, girlie, where ya been?"

The chorus of dormitory girls at her doorway chirped their greetings with pink-faced smiles.

"It's like every time I knock on your door you're not here!"

Stepping shoeless into the hallway, Saleema moved through the girls and toward the vending machine. A Diet Coke and a thirty-five-cent bag of Linden's Butter Crunch cookies, like from the bodega at home.

"Hey, Saleema! *Hey girl, hey*!" A freshman offered a too-wide smile and an eager wave as Saleema walked down the steps toward the front door.

"Wazz-*up*, Saleema? I tried to call you. Is your phone, like, not working?" This one, who lived in the room next door to Saleema, had stolen her last St. Ides Special Brew a week earlier, passed out drunk on the hallway in front of her door, and had said nothing to her since.

Saleema acknowledged the girls' greetings with a vague smile that she hoped communicated disinterest—though if it didn't, she resolved, today she really didn't care. She grabbed her pea coat from the foyer, slid the soda into one pocket and the cookies into the other, looked down at her shoeless feet, and left the building.

Outside, sweeping afternoon shadows made the brick campus look fragile and falsely meticulous, like an architect's cardboard model or a movie set. But when she stepped away from the dorm, the sun filtered through her lashes and hit her cheeks with the soft sting she had always loved to feel at home. She smiled at the air, and when she saw the southbound Blue Line bus across the street, she got on.

The people on the bus watched, as always, while Saleema lumbered through the narrow door and up the three steep steps. Today, she watched them back.

"Free ride," said the driver, a stone-faced Latina woman with soft-looking skin. Saleema imagined that her smile, when coaxed, must be wide.

A little white boy with colored pencils in his hands stared at her as she moved up the aisle, his eyes huge and unblinking, as though she were a new kind of creature in a Saturday cartoon.

A white lady with thick eyebrows and a bolt of silver hair looked at Saleema's feet, then turned toward the window and scowled, her face beautiful and severe.

A dreadlocked woman in the middle of the bus looked at Saleema's stomach, frowned, then clasped her fingers over her own stomach, her many rings tinkling.

A young guy with pink hair in the handicap seat looked at Saleema's shoeless feet and nodded, then he rubbed his face and turned quickly back to his Discman before Saleema had a chance to smile at him.

Saleema was used to feeling like a strange, brown spot in peoples' daily commute. But today it didn't matter. She smiled at each of them. These people did not need to know that this spot could gaze, could read their disquieted faces, and be completely in love anyway.

That was the nice thing about love. She had thought about it a lot the night before as and that girl read excerpts from *Temple of My Familiar*, smoke tumbling like pixie dust in the air between them. Love, didn't have to make sense to anyone, especially the person doing the loving. All you owed it was to let it be. And sometimes, it didn't even need to be— sometimes, just the possibility was enough.

In her favorite seat in the back corner of the bus, she put her bare feet up and began to sing a medley of Janet Jackson songs quietly to herself, and to anyone who cared to listen. Lost in the rapture and glide of "When I Think of You," she had not noticed the small man a few rows up who had risen from his seat and was now walking toward her. His shoelaces were untied and he wore a dried powder blue carnation on his lapel. His eyes were clear and glazed like glass marbles, and his cheeks and brow shone as though he were about to greet an old friend. As he approached, Saleema noticed that he smelled faintly of rotten oranges. Since she was a child, her mother had liked to leave orange peels on the stove to scent the kitchen, and this smell had always reminded her of home. And so when the man extended his hand, she took it.

"Can't wait, eh?" He thudded into the seat in front of her. She moved her feet and nodded, loving this strange man's appearance.

He rubbed his face, then tapped the silver handrail as he spoke. "It's like I always said—better to just wait and see. Always hard though, y'know?"

Saleema looked at the man and waited for more. He paused and gazed at a cough syrup ad overhead. Then he jerked suddenly and faced Saleema with imploring eyes.

"I'll never leave again. Now, say what they want, these crazies will, but I'd rather stay where I know, now that I know. That last push outta mama's tum-tum, you watch. Every baby—the president and his shit cleaner—they 'cry cause they wanna get back in. I say stay where y'know, or find it where y'go, if y'can." He shook his head slowly as though in pain and closed his eyes.

The lovely, mean white lady was now standing, clasped to the silver pole by the back door. She caught Saleema in an accidental glance that was startling at first, but then made Saleema want to laugh. The woman had known immediately that this big, shoeless black girl was a shame—and now look at the company she was keeping! By the time the last puff of feathers from the woman's unseasonable winter coat had floated down to the bus floor, Saleema's strange companion was asleep.

At school, the dormitory girls wondered where Saleema had gone so abruptly on a Saturday afternoon—and without any shoes on at that. The told each other they hoped Saleema hadn't been nabbed by lunatics, but in truth, they weren't convinced such vulnerability was possible for her, even in their wildest imaginations.

Saleema sang "Escapade" more quietly, so as not to disturb the sleeper.

It wasn't until the driver called Sovereign Street that Saleema noticed no other stop had been announced along the ride. Hearing the driver's voice, the sleeping man rose and flew off the bus in one quick motion, without a glance in Saleema's direction. Saleema was disappointed. He had engaged her in his bizarre conversation, fallen asleep on her, and then left unexpectedly, without even a strange or silent good-bye.

Everyone at home would have rolled their eyes, shaken their heads, and given her a mouthful of reasons to let her moment with the man end there. But the feeling of that girl's smoke—the curiosity, the excitement, the wondering-what-could-be—won out in the end. She fastened her coat, pressed the yellow tape by the back door, and gazed up at the driver's rear view mirror, begging with her eyes for the doors to open again.

Coolness and the setting sun made Sovereign Street a hard, gray place, and the man was nowhere in sight. After walking down the blocks for a few minutes, the soda in her pocket began to chill her thigh and her toes started to feel dead and numb. She tried to find a heated spot to warm her feet, but there were no steaming manholes or subway grates here—only clean, even pavement stretching uninterrupted for blocks. On one corner, she saw a penny winking from the ground.

This was probably the best this adventure would offer her, she decided, and perhaps it wasn't all that bad. It was almost definitely unwise to follow eccentric white men down unknown streets, but found pennies could be good. At home, the rhyme was: *Find a penny, pick it up, all day long you got good luck.* In junior high, several other versions of the rhyme cropped up: *Find a penny, pick it up, wish that it had been a buck*; *Find a penny, pick it up, tell your moms she really sucks*, and, Saleema's favorite, *Find a penny, pick it up, lose that shit, who gives a fuck? It's a fucking penny!* If she didn't find the man, she reasoned, the penny would be a cute moment in her year's best day. And if she did find him, some luck might come in handy. And so she reached down.

Across the street, a little boy wrote curse words on the ground in blue chalk, smiling toothily in Saleema's direction.

Back at the dormitory, Saleema's disappearance was no longer a topic of conversation; mid-terms and Saturday evening affairs were at hand.

Stooping for the penny, she saw a flash out the corner of her eye—a quick glint of something down moving the alley beside her. She pocketed the penny and moved closer. Finally, she saw the man sitting on the front stairs of an abandoned building, his back hunched over and his elbows on his knees like a seasoned stoop-sitter from home.

She stopped at a mailbox and fiddled with the handle, eyeing the man. But as soon as she paused he stood, jerked around, and sailed further down the block with a smooth, important stride. Saleema walked a few yards behind him. It was clear now—if it hadn't been before: infatuation and homesickness were overwhelming her good sense. She observed the fact like a scene unfolding on a TV screen, imagining what folks from home would say, but continuing all the same. When the man entered a huge teal-colored building and held the huge steel doors open behind him, huge Saleema followed right in.

The room did not even smell like oranges. That was the only real surprise.

It did not surprise her that they all looked like him, bore his same height and weight, same attire with slight variations. She was not surprised by the impeccable congruence of their matching carnations—this one lavender, that one paisley, this one polka-dotted and aquamarine. The ceilings were beanstalk high, and the walls seemed to hum with the men's tangled, throaty chatter as they all worked diligently at small blue machines. It was breathtaking and perfect. They were Dorothy's munchkins, Alice's playing cards, and Saleema was not surprised at all.

Standing in the doorway, Saleema saw that the walls were lined with large bails filled almost to the brim with mounds of a white, grainy substance that looked like flour but smelled like the sweet baby powder that girls always wore in the summer at home. The powder poured from the tube at the end of each little blue machine into a series of small cylindrical vats on the floor. Men with black-and-white speckled carnations drove tall carts up and down the aisles collecting the vats, filling the carts with powder, and leaving a thin white fog behind them as they went.

Watching, Saleema remembered home. She remembered the sandwich bags full of white powder that she carried around the streets of Harlem for eight months of the ninth grade, concealed in a hole in her coat. She remembered delighting in the soft, sandy texture of the powder every chance she got, rolling it lightly between her fingertips, clenching it tight and full in her fists, then releasing it slowly through the cracks between her fingers, *smiling-in* as she did last night with each breath of that girl's smoke.

The playground on Amsterdam Avenue was always dark indigo in Saleema's memory, and it always smelled like plátanos and chocolate thai with slow breeze and fast lights. The dented metal slides that burned bare legs in the summer and the broken tire swings beside them remembered like home, and the Saleema's powder was part of that. She remembered questioning the gravelly cement benches that prickled thighs and the single chess tables that joined them, wondering who thought neighborhood people would sit and play chess in pairs in the playground when there was each other and home to engage.

The coco helado man and the hot dog lady should marry when we are jumping double-dutch my mama your mama sitting on the fence and loving powder because it is so soft and so texture turned into an adjective the texturest superlative and she was the only one who knew what it meant but she was not the only one who knew what it was at home playing house in the jungle gym and wondering why there was room for a jungle down the street from the stoop where every day was a block party in blue mood and little girls would steal your my little pony to bring on your first

*fight at home in the playground still loving that
powder and being the only one when you leave and go
to a smart people school a white people school and
talk like you do and look like you do and can still
teddy bear teddy bear turn around teddy bear teddy
bear touch the ground... saleema will remember shug
and celie's song and see it in herself and her girls will
see the movie and remember saleema and they'll
wonder where saleema is now.*

*saleema is inside of white powder where she lives
and where she is from under the lights that who-knew-
how they came up early in the winter and late in the
summer in the corners by the fence where the red ants
were and you betta not step on the cracks cuz if you
did all the girls would giggle as you giggled she
giggled saleema did when the old man pissed on the
basketball court after the church women had gone
home to cook for the week and do someone's hair and
How you doing baby and Did you want some food and
Where is your mother working hard, Lord Jesus,
hardheaddedness was enough to urge her into pussy
and smoke and love and home like powder and
everyone knew her powder and her were deep and
close like home and everyone knew where that was but
not everyone knew what it meant Throw yo shit yo/
throw yo shit, saleema when five-o comes they wont
care bout the difference between powder and snow,
blow, yeya yo ass is crazy but they ain't us don't know
you love you like home like that girl throw yo shit we
smokin weed and you got powder in your pocket girl
don't you know you could get us caught like eeney
meeney miney mo catch us they will catch us girl... yo
powder can get us killed.*

Saleema held her braids to her nose and sniffed for the smoke in the rain in front of the building. She pulled them, twisted them, wrung them around themselves and inhaled desperately, but she could not find the smell and there was no powder outside. She wanted to fall on her bed and feel home on her skin but she was in the middle of noplace and her skin was too wet to feel.

When she got back, the dormitory was dank and the girls were preparing for a party.

"Whazz-*up*, Saleema?"

"Yeah, girlie! Where'd you go?"

"No shoes today, huh, Saleema? Hehe!"

Saleema sat on the front steps and held her head as the girls shuffled past her, in and out of the rain. She stayed that way until the moon was bright platinum against an inky sky, and then she moved inside.

She should have grown used to having big realizations at her most naked times. This one had come years before and sporadically since, over tops of silky heads in subway cars, in unyielding lecture hall chairs, in photographs, and in front of bedroom mirrors. Now she was sitting, clothed and soggy, on the closed toilet in a narrow stall when she presented herself with the fact: she was not a woman. She was too big and too black and too full of something thicker than blood to be a person at all.

She took the soda and the cookies from her coat pocket and placed them on the bathroom floor. At the sink, she watched herself: dark-lined lips that sang home in mattress commercials, bright green nails as strange in New England as they were in New York. Round cheeks that drank the sun when they could and *smiled in*. She washed her hands thoroughly—three times, maybe four—wishing for lather to make powder and water to make smoke so she would feel at home again. She stood there for full minutes with that wish, heart bouncing like a girl yearning to leap in to a twirling clothesline for double-dutch, unsure if it would ever be her turn.

In the foyer, Saleema dialed her campus voice mail and listened to "Big Poppa" play behind her on the outgoing greeting.

"What up, y'all, this is Saleema. Leave a message. Peace." Her voice was thick and steady like syrup, she thought—a lie. Standing amid the chatting girls, the party-planning banter, she entered her pin number and waited for her one new message to play.

"Now, bitch, you know we was just bumpin' Biggie in the room so now you wanna throw some mufuckin' Big Poppa on your voicemail? Aight then. But yo, where you at? I'm just chillin', wondering what's going on with you—haven't seen you since, like, this morning. Anyway, I'm 'bout to smoke me a cigarette. Holla back. Love you, girl. One."

Saleema's skin was warm. She closed her eyes, smiled, and breathed deep.

A Strange People

We-Chrissie will let the white men see and touch our difference. She will smile for doctors and handlers like Mrs. Susan's old china trinket dolls, tilt her head just so and laugh, her hand grabbing at our hemline. In the next town, we'll see banners and broadsides proclaiming our "charm." We-Millie will not understand why they would write us that way. She will taste the words like coffee grounds in her mouth and wonder how they can print them so small and neat below the headlines: "Double-Headed Darkey," "United Negress Freaks," "Two-Headed African Beast." We-Chrissie will not have these questions. She will know that the nice words are for her. She is the one who has always hated us.

When we were young, decades ago, We-Chrissie wrote her version of our story, and everyone who knew us was surprised. She got most of the facts straight, told about our slave birth and the scandal we caused on our first master's farm, how we were sold from Master John and Mrs. Susan, then slipped like a wet hunk of soap from hand to hand, master to master, growing up and filling out the carnival circuit. She told how we saw things most North Carolina nigger girls wouldn't even think to dream of—the darting English steam cars, the white-choked winter at the Cirque des Champs-Elysées. We-Chrissie spent a few words on We-Millie's favorite part of the life, when we ended up back in Mrs. Susan's arms. She said a couple of things about our life on the midway, the place between the circus gates and the big top, where freak acts wander about and ballyhoo, squeezing awe from the norms' eyes like milk from fat cows' udders.

We-Chrissie is an all-star bally, always has been. She preened and flaunted in her story too, playing our difference up and down to suit her audience. First it was a "malformation," then it was a "joy." Our join was a curse we were proud of, she said, writing on our minds the paradox of our body. She refused to let them think for a second that the slightest drip of difference ran between we-two. "We are indeed a strange people," she began her story, and it continued on like that—"a people," two, but one. She refused to tell anyone that it was she alone who had written the story, without letting We-Millie so much as touch the pen or smell the ink when the manuscript was done. We-Chrissie wrote, then—and will tell anyone who asks now—that there is only one heart in the body. We-Millie sits silent when she says this, and lets her go ahead with her show. We-Millie knows, though, that our hearts are separate. Our wombs, our backs, our hot puddles and buttons come in and out of each other like corset laces; We-Chrissie feels We-Millie's itches and We-Millie rubs on We-Chrissie's aches, but for We-Millie, our hearts are separate things, different as the sun and the moon pinning down the ends of a long day's sky.

It is obvious to everyone that We-Chrissie is the charming one. She is the one the newspapers talk about when they say we are beautiful. We-Millie is the one that scares people, we think. She is quiet and unsure, and if we were not us—if we were norms, or nigger girls at least—We-Millie would never find herself anywhere near a stage. We-Millie speaks German and Spanish better than We-Chrissie, better than Mrs. Susan, who taught us. But she stays quiet, the small, silent half. We-Chrissie is stronger; We-Millie is frail. We-Chrissie is pretty; We-Millie is darker and with a gnarling nose. When We-Chrissie smiles at the doctors and invites them to probe the body, We-Millie plays along and feels her mouth burn with quiet. It is her feebler puddle, her crookeder pit in which they will splash and plunge to their hearts' content.

While We-Chrissie talks to reporters, doctors, and midway norms, We-Millie moves her mouth and smiles along, but sends her mind inside. Both of we-two make up stories. We-Chrissie likes to say hers, shout them out from the stage, write them down in books. We-Millie keeps her stories to herself.

When Mrs. Susan heard about We-Chrissie's story, she smiled, her soft pink cheeks glowing as she chuckled. "You couldn't have convinced me that *that* one ever learned to read." She pointed her chin at We-Chrissie. "Least not by my hand. Don't know what you-all picked up on the road, I suppose."

We-Chrissie was never bothered by Mrs. Susan's comments. We-Millie couldn't get enough of Mrs. Susan, but We-Chrissie always her in sips, swishing her around in slow judgment whenever she was around, spitting her name out bitterly when it was just we-two alone.

The biggest fight we ever had happened the morning of Master John's funeral. We-Chrissie wanted to wear our star-spangled taffeta costume to the service. She said we'd be the blow-off, the grand finale of Master John's long-lived show. To her, he was a freak on his own, and a gaff—a liar—at that. She said he passed for a kind master, an innocent pushed into managing us by altruism and Christian duty, but that he was really a mastermind who had plotted our course from our birth, calculating our life's revenue by the time we were two months old. We-Millie liked her skepticism, but got hot at the thought of disrespecting Mrs. Susan by wearing the dress. We-Millie has loved Mrs. Susan forever, in the way that norm women, she thinks, love the people who take care of them, make them feel like the secret of life lives between their two limbs.

We-Chrissie loved our midway life, and We-Millie liked it well enough too. Although it was clotted with people and noise, We-Millie enjoyed the camaraderie that came with a traveling pack of freaks. Zip Johnson, "The What-Is-It," adopted us as his niece, and would visit our tent in his furry brown costume after his "missing link" show, spinning us around in pirouettes and sharing some of the bananas he was paid to hurl at his audiences. Bearded and fat ladies of all heights and temperaments mothered us, pressing our hair and teaching us how to send our minds away from the body when norm men came to us with their pointing parts and oily smiles. For We-Millie, Miss Ella Ewing, the Missouri Giantess, was heaven itself, and the nook between her chest and her yardstick arm was a personal paradise. Miss Ella had traveled with Buffalo Bill's Wild West Show, and it had filled her with stories we could listen to for days. We-Chrissie loved to hear about the high, steady pay Miss Ella received, and the handsome Indian men she performed with. We-Millie simply liked the sad, deep moan of the giantess's voice. We-Millie dragged the body to her every chance she got, just to curl into the nook of her chest and hear her thunderstorm breath, her earthquake heartbeat.

We-Chrissie has always insisted that we have no real family, though she didn't write that in her book. We-Millie sees it differently. For her, the circus folks—the midway freaks and the staff, the managers' wives and children, and sometimes men like Barnum himself—make a collage of a family portrait we can hang proudly enough on the wall of our life. We-Chrissie's face sours when We-Millie says these things, and she spits. "You also insist on thinking that the man who sold us to the stage loves you." We-Millie thinks *Yes, I have to think that, and I have to think he loves you too.* But she doesn't need to say it, of course, because We-Chrissie knows.

Mrs. Susan and Master John hold our story together like bookends—we both agree on that. They were there when life set us whirling about like a spinning top, and here they are again—the lady and the ghost—now that things are starting to slow down. Master John was still living when he and Mrs. Susan came to England to get us from Lars Rachman, the most recent man to have crept into a tent and stolen us in the middle of the night. Master John was brusque as usual, but kind enough, returning We-Chrissie's buttermilk smile as he ushered us out of the Liverpool courtroom. Mrs. Susan was slower, warmer, as was her way. She held her arms out and called our names, pulling the body toward her with her scent and her feel and her promise of home.

We were too young to know then that home doesn't exist unless it's far from you, that either it or you must disappear the moment you return. North Carolina was decimated after the Civil War, and by then Master John's house was no more a home than a floor plank was a blacktop. We-Millie is sure it was the shock of our return and the swollen weight of Mrs. Susan's misery that first brought the fever to her side of the body. We-Chrissie has always laughed those claims off, not so much to dismiss her as to keep her focused on the tasks at hand. Master John died of gout before We-Millie had a chance to feel all of her pain, and our status as breadwinners for his family and for ourselves became official.

We-Chrissie became our manager, making contacts with the North Carolina showmen we'd known before we left, dazzling them all with her smile and her laugh, running her bally to keep them interested. Her act was tight and she always got her *ding*, as circus folks say, the clink of whatever capital against whatever pot she passed around. We needed money, of course, but We-Chrissie was smart. She knew that a few dollars weekly from a traveling sideshow gig was alright for a pair of young nigger-girl freaks without the need or right to do for themselves, but we were grown, almost old, and as free as we would ever be. We needed money, We-

Chrissie knew, but it was information that would make us. We needed to know what opportunities we could find—or drum up for ourselves—on the nation's larger stage. We-Chrissie enlisted the help of Ron Samuel, Master John's old stableman, and set the body flitting about the marshlands of Columbus County with her ear to the tracks of the circus world, dropping Master John's good name like maple sugar candies whenever we needed white norm protection.

It was in a saloon near Soule's Swamp that we heard the news We-Chrissie thought would change our life. The barmaid was a woman who had ballyhooed for P.T. Barnum's show years before, when we were being billed as the "Two-Headed Cherub Monstrosity." She was a kind woman with a ruddy face and a mess of wheat-colored hair piled up on her head. She always liked Master John and Mrs. Susan, and We-Millie thought she was nice enough to us, though We-Chrissie insisted she was simply trying to get on Master John's good side, which for her meant the inside of his pants. Still, the woman smiled when we shuffled sideways through the door, and offered us a glass of lemonade, which We-Millie decided we would drink.

"You girls know 'bout the nigger show?" the woman asked, watching We-Chrissie's face for evidence that she felt or tasted the lemonade. We-two shook our heads.

"Man behind Buffalo Bill and the Wild West show—not Cody, but the money man, a Yankee. He's doing a big show about niggers. You-all'd be perfect for it."

We-Millie could feel We-Chrissie's smile spread on the skin. We-Chrissie thanked the woman and yanked the body toward the door so quickly We-Millie had to pinch the spine to slow us down so she could pay. The woman smiled, and We-Millie felt her eyes on the body as we ambled out the door, We-Millie glad to be heading home as always, We-Chrissie dreaming of New York City, plotting the course of our life anew.

The first thing Nate Salsbury saw as he stepped toward his office door, a hot mug of coffee in his hand, was the shadow of what looked like a lightening-struck bonsai tree hovering on his wall. The dark shape startled him, then drew him in. He paused at the doorway and gripped his mug, trying not to drop the mug or spill the coffee, as he'd felt scattered and off-kilter since his morning meeting. But as the shadow began to twirl along the wall, practicing its audition dance, he assumed, he decided to sip for a moment and watch the figure move. A perfect bonsai, he determined: mangled even in its symmetry, purely exotic, fine and lovely and no less than grotesque. As the creature rose and began to twist, he walked toward it, slowly catching its rhythm, hurriedly catching his breath.

"I heard you were a dancer," he said, setting the mug beside his leather blotter. "But I could never have dreamed a figure of such brilliant grace."

It couldn't be called a beautiful creature, exactly, but there was something enthralling, almost fetching about it. It stood five feet tall, with four legs and four arms, but only one forked, double-wide torso, which seemed curve in on itself in a twiglike construction, giving it the look of two young girls pressed back-to-back in a game of peek-a-boo.

71

The creature smiled with its slightly prettier head and halted, one half dipping into a curtsey, which the other half mirrored perfectly.

"How can we respond to a compliment from a man so discerning and worldly as yourself?" the fairer head said. "We can only invite you to examine us as long and as fully as your least whim would have."

Salsbury smiled, taken aback by the pointedness of the creature's charm. This head was clearly the showman, he concluded, and the businessman as well. The other head was engaged, nodding and smiling throughout, but it seemed to maintain a certain distance, watching the scene carefully but saying almost nothing.

He had heard about this creature, touted as a Negress version of the two-headed Oriental that had made such a splash on the circuit some years ago. The comparison was logical, of course, but seeing this creature before him, he saw that that description missed much. The fairer head in particular had a clawing spunk that even the more animated half of the Oriental could never have aspired to. She had the bite of any Negro woman made tough and mannish by years of work, yet too smart to relinquish the last dregs of her femininity. Other things about the creature, though, he had never seen in a Negro, or an Indian, or talent of any kind before. This being before him seemed to see itself just as a showman would see it, locating the lair of its dark allure and subduing its other parts to keep all eyes on the money spot. The creature bent its two inner legs leisurely and fanned a smile, awaiting his response.

"Well, Miss McKoy, I am obviously honored by

your offer," he said, settling in behind his desk. "But of course you'd want to know your talents were fully appreciated before having them committed to the whim, as you say, of a stranger. I hear that among your many gifts is a literary talent. Is that right?"

The creature nodded its heads, and the sullen face seemed to brighten up.

"Oh yes," the fair head said eagerly. "We know the best parts of Spenser and many of the sonnets, as well as the major works of Molinet, and du Mans, along with all of the Lay of Hildebrand, each in the original language, and in translation, of course."

"And," the plain head interrupted dryly, "we compose our own poetry as well."

"Yes," he sighed, leaning back. "I'd be delighted to hear an original composition from the very four lips of the poetess."

The creature opened its mouths, offering for the first time a taste of their vocal harmony. Salsbury had expected some tonal dissonances, as one often heard in the first few seconds of duo or group auditions. But the creature made no false starts. It launched flawlessly into a compelling rhymed bit about its life, its two voices perfectly pitched and ringing clearly as a single bell.

As the creature spoke, Salsbury recalled the morning's meeting. He had had in this same office what initially impressed as an unremarkable group, also auditioning for his Negro show, which would go up at the Third Avenue Theatre at the end of they year. He had put word out weeks before among colleagues and busybodies that he was assembling history's largest Negro performance, to match ticket for ticket and dollar for dollar his success with Buffalo Bill, and to exceed the Wild West show in quality as well as moral heft. This exhibition, he had told them all, would showcase the finer qualities of the Negro. It would bring to the fore the darker race's evolution from African jungle savagery to New York civilization, and would recall all the delights of the Negro's character at each stage. The advertisements would mention the Negro's darker days, but would also herald his resurrection. Audiences the world over would be thrilled by all parts of the spectacle. They would cull joy from the Negro's triumph, and be relieved from their own pains by the utterly black drama unfolding on stage.

Salsbury had to acknowledge that it was a brilliant idea each time he thought about it. It was going perfectly, and after only two months of planning, the first performance was nearly cast. The best minstrel actors had been recruited from all along the eastern seaboard, and New York's highest-grossing stage writers were at work on scripts that would bring the high drama of the Negro's history to the stage. He was now in the more relaxed phase of booking specialty acts. As well as things had gone up to this point, the moment in which he found himself now was a strange one. Here he was, requiring himself to choose between this Negress freak, an embodiment of error, and the ostensibly unremarkable group he had seen this morning. And even as the cloven creature sparkled eerily before him, reading what was turning out to be a shockingly competent poem, he found himself pulled toward this morning's less-than-spectacle, a group called That So Different Four.

He had expected the group to shuffle into his office at least five minutes late, as was the Negro way. His first surprise, then, was to find them dressed to the nines and reading newspapers casually beside his secretary's desk when he walked in to the office, twenty minutes before their appointment time of ten o'clock. The surprise did not end there—rather, it grew into shock as he heard the group speak and watched them perform. The two men and two women moved as a unit, and spoke as clearly and articulately as the creature before him, which, in a way, made the freestanding Negroes even more remarkable. The two-headed creature was made, sent even, to thrill and bewilder. But a pack of well-dressed, well-spoken, unsmiling darkies, mannered and reading, operating together with an almost mechanical precision—this was the kind of spectacle no audience could forget. The two-headed Negro girl would alarm audiences, for sure. But the dandies—no, not dandies, one couldn't really even call them that—the "Different" negroes, with their seriousness and their finery just on the slight side of decadence, would bring the audiences to their edge. Their act was not the childish mockery that proliferated on the minstrel stage, though they certainly had the innate musical talent typical of their race. Still, save for their color, this group had almost all the airs of normal, modern men. An act like that was striking in a powerful, nearly sinister way. The "Different" Negro ensemble would haunt audiences as they haunted him now, their dark eyes flashing from wall placards, campaign posters, family portraits on parlor walls, or worse—and chillingly better—from the looking glass itself. The thought scared and thrilled him, and he found himself eager to see them at a distance, behind the fourth wall of the stage. They were performers, niggers in the theater like so many; and yet unlike the minstrels—and unlike the odd lump of flesh that sat before him now—the So Different Four were not so different at all. They were black, of course, but otherwise, they were nearly…

When the creature's poem concluded, the prettier head gave a confident, expectant smile, pushing her side of its chest toward him.

"Well, you certainly are talented," Salsbury said. He stood and walked toward the creature. "Surely no one could be disappointed by such a treat. Thank you for your time, young lad—" He stammered, unsure whether to the plural was appropriate, or if the singular was right. Instead, he put his hand on the creature's back, making sure to get a grab of the fleshy, wishbone spine as he ushered it out the door.

We stayed on in New York for three weeks after our meeting with Salsbury, in a property of Mrs. Amanda Bunting, a friend of Mrs. Susan's. Mrs. Bunting owned a boarding house on the southeast tip of the city, in the middle of a cluster of settlement houses, slaughterhouses, and Jewish bakeries. The building was empty, as Mrs. Bunting and her husband had just bought the property and had yet to carve it up into single rooms. Mrs. Bunting lived far across the city—a chess knight's move away, she said—and so there was no sense in feeding the coal stove daily just to keep our one body warm. Still, she promised us privacy and discretion at the boarding house, and, for the most part, delivered both. We lived off of money

Mrs. Susan loaned us, though We-Chrissie refused to call it a loan—all of Mrs. Susan's money, she said, came from us at the end of the day.

We spent our time in New York gazing out of Mrs. Bunting's garden-parlor window at the feet of norms, watching their heels pass in pairs nimbly over the cobblestones. We-Millie felt a quick tug from We-Chrissie's side of the body when one of the new electrified streetcars passed by; We-Chrissie was excited by the cars' speed and smoothness. She talked about how grand it would be to be perched in one of those seats, darting sleekly from one glamorous place to another as we prepared for our debut in Salsbury's show. We-Millie shuddered under Mrs. Bunting's blankets when We-Chrissie's said these things. We-Millie's chills and fevers had worsened since we'd arrived in New York. Her side of the body seemed to grow frailer and weaker with each new day, but We-Chrissie did not notice, or if she did, she did not seem to care.

When we didn't hear from Salsbury after a week, We-Chrissie asked Mrs. Bunting to load us in her carriage and carry us back to his office, a mile away up on Tin Pan Alley, where we waited with his secretary for two hours before being told he wouldn't be able to see us that day. It was a cool, wet afternoon, the kind we have only experienced in the American North, where the wind feels mean and lazy at once, and the rain seems to pinch at the skin, as though to get its attention. Finally, the chills began to spread to We-Chrissie's side of the body, and, now feeling them too, We-Chrissie promised that we would return to Columbus County as soon as we signed a contract for the Negro show. Once signed, she said, we would stay home with Mrs. Susan until just before the opening performance, but not a day longer.

Leaving Salsbury's building, we stopped near the entranceway to fumble with our umbrellas, trying to make sure sure to cover the join. We-Millie had turned to protect her hair from a big gust of droplets when the finest group of niggers we had ever seen waltzed toward Salsbury's building. At the head of the pack was a tall, slim brown man with eyes like pools of sweetmilk and lashes as long as a foxtail's fur. We-Millie felt a rush of blood through the body, and We-Chrissie lurched so quickly toward the man that We-Millie worried, for a second, that the join might tear.

His name, it turned out, was Carlo. He was the lead performer of a new musical group being courted to join Salsbury's show. We-Chrissie gave Carlo a smile We-Millie had never felt before, one that buzzed over the entire surface of the body and burrowed into the knots of our flesh. Both of we-two watched the young women in the group, though We-Millie eyed them only long enough to see that neither of them looked kind. They were tall—taller even than most norm women—and they both dressed finely, in smart streetcoats with silver buckles and shiny, pointed shoes. To We-Millie, they were long and slick and glassy-looking, like Mrs. Susan's bud vases, their bodies curving in and out with perfect symmetry, their shoulders reaching up into the air as though poised to receive a gift.

We-two felt instantly ashamed, though we were wearing the best costume we had—a black and blue suede number with beadwork and embroidery that cinched our waist. We felt the women's eyes fall on the body, saw the familiar mix of nausea and awe on their faces. We-Millie wanted to leave the scene, to find dryness and warmth somewhere and wrap the body in it, fast. But We-Chrissie wanted to stay, and so we did, We-Chrissie talking and preening while We-Millie shivered in the rain. After a while, We-Chrissie determined that the two women were Carlo's colleagues and nothing more. This meant something important to We-Chrissie, in a way that We-Millie only half-understood.

Carlo said that he had heard about our act as a child, and had thought of us as icons as he dreamed about an entertainment career. This news fell on We-Chrissie like a marriage vow, and she began to gush compliments over him, being sure to work in details of our life that would indicate—in case he was too simple to know, We-Millie thought—that we were single and available. We-Millie gave him Mrs. Bunting's address and suggested that he call on us to chat about our experience in the business, or anything else that might spark his interest. He thanked her with a deep bow and proceeded with his company out of the rain, leaving us to the task of keeping ourselves dry and giving us another call to wait for.

The following morning, We-Millie's fever broke like a cloud into sweat showers, and the coughs from her side of the body began to produce a pinkish phlegm. Still, We-Chrissie added days to our stay in the North, insisting that Salsbury, or Carlo, or somebody, would call on us at any minute.

We-Millie finds it needless to say that neither call ever came. We-Chrissie resents this feeling from the body's other half.

What is remarkable, for We-Millie at least, is the course our story was taking, even as we dallied in New York, holding ourself up for sale like the last rotting piece of fruit at the produce market. What is remarkable, even We-Chrissie won't deny, is the shock, still with us, of returning to Columbus on a Saturday morning—with no contract and no one having called—to be met with Ron Samuel's stricken face and shattered voice, announcing in an auctioneer's bewildered monotone how Mrs. Susan passed, alone, soaked with sweat, late the night before.

We did not know something like this could happen. We-Chrissie did not know how painful it can be to get one's way. We-Millie did not know how one's own will, discarded, can fly back to hurt the people one loves. We-Millie tries not to think how differently things may have gone if we-two had come back earlier—how perhaps the body might not be drowning in fever as it is now, how perhaps we might have gotten Mrs. Susan to a doctor in time to keep her alive.

We-Chrissie will say there was no way of knowing Mrs. Susan was ill, that she didn't know how bad We-Millie's fevers had grown. We-Millie will know these are the kind of lies told only to soothe the liar. What we both knew well was men like Salsbury. We knew him like we have known all the masters and handlers and doctors, all the white norm men, all our lives. We should have been used to wordless rejection. We should not have been surprised by his. We-Chrissie felt his ambivalence as he eyed the body, even while we spun around his office, doing our most difficult dance. We-Millie felt him stare at us as though he expected gold coins to pour from between our legs, smelled his disappointment when they did not. But we needed money as badly as Salsbury wanted it. So We-Millie stayed quiet while We-Chrissie brightened her face and stuck out her bosom, waving the body in the white man's face like a flag before a firing squad.

We-Millie tries to be understanding as she remembers. She tries not to think of Mrs. Susan, just as We-Chrissie tries not to think of Carlo, the nigger show, and all the other things she feels we've lost.

"We were stupid to think they would always want us," We-Chrissie sighs, her head falling onto We-Millie's shoulder. "We were silly to believe we could be just the right blend of bile and sugar always. That tastes and people would not change and leave us here in this torture box, alone. How stupid we were…"

You were stupid. The thought slices like a knife through the body.

You were stupid to think they wanted you in the first place. You were dumb to let your fantasies eat you. *You* are the stupid one. *You.* Alone. I have never been your twin.

The shoulders twist. The heads roll apart. We are sharing a brutal wish.

The back hands reach for each other and stroke themselves. A hot sweat slicks up on the spine, a chill rushes down from the tender crevice of the join. We have never shared this wish before.

We-Chrissie's heart is slowing. We-Millie feels hers quicken.

Saturday

The truth was, Malaya Clondon had been thinking of French fries since last night, as she ate Chinese food in secret with her father while her mother worked late at the university. The thought of French fries stayed with her through the canned laughter and blonde-headed family tableaus of the Friday night sitcom lineup, and helped her push herself from the bed most Saturday mornings. She thought of the shiny fried strips, nested together, boasting countless shades of yellow and gold, from the time she and her mother left their brownstone in the morning till she felt, at last, the film of hot grease on her face after dance class, so much later in the day.

On the walk to the meeting, other foods drifted to mind. Trailing behind her mother, Malaya would prod herself to gallop quickly past the delicious smells of Harlem, willing herself not to notice them. Malaya and Professor Clondon passed at least eight bodegas on the walk, plus the McDonald's and the Kentucky Fried, and the Woolworth's on Broadway, where the smell of hot popcorn seemed to seep from beneath the glass doors in slow waves. On 145th Street there was Copeland's, where they made crispy smothered chicken with gravy as thick as pudding and potato salad that was perfectly sweet and salty at once. But by the time they pushed through the heavy green doors of A.M.E. Mt. Canaan Church and went down to the basement community center where the meeting was held—by the time Malaya took her turn on the scale and watched red numbers blink and multiply beneath her, feeling her mother's eyes fixed on the number panel from behind—Malaya thought only of the salty-sweet potato-and-ketchup-crusted mush she would have just before art class. She did not think of the hour of dance she would have to get through beforehand, or of what lie she would tell about how her allowance had been spent.

"Well, don't everybody speak up at once now!" Ms. Adelaide, the meeting leader, said, laughing over the collar of her lavender suit.

Malaya watched the woman walk to the front of the room, which was full of fat women on folding chairs. Ms. Adelaide caressed her plastic easel, flipping back a page marked "EMOTIONAL TRIGGERS PIE CHART," and exposing a sheet as clean and white as the face of a new tub of Cool Whip. She stood there, her hip sloped prettily out before her, her arms loose and easy along her waist.

"Come on, ladies. Don't be shy." She shifted into another breathtakingly casual pose, resting her weight on one tall plumb-colored high heel and letting a hand float up to stroke the paper. "I want you to think about your favorite food. You know we all have that one food that always gets us in trouble. Well now, I want you to think about it. Call it out!"

Malaya listened, catching a few coughs, small

squeakings of the metal seats. She glanced up at her mother. Professor Clondon always sat a seat away from Malaya at the meeting, balancing her pocketbook and briefcase against her hip on the seat between them and leaving room for Malaya to do the same with her Hello-Kitty Saturday bag. Malaya was never sure who had begun this arrangement—she or her mother—or if it was something they had agreed on, silently, together. Either way, after a year of attending the meetings, Malaya decided she didn't mind the distance, not really. It gave her space to spread her papers and colored pencils out on her lap and pretend she wasn't there.

Ms. Adelaide took a breath, awaiting the women's response, but the room stayed quiet. The rustling of papers somewhere in the back of the room brought saltwater to Malaya's mouth as she thought of removing an order French fries from their wax paper covering. She imagined the brown and orange and yellow strips bending over one another in a red-and-white striped paper dish, a shower of salt crystals hitting them from all sides and sparkling on them like glitter.

"Alright, now. I know it can be embarrassing," Ms. Adelaide said.

She leaned back, posed, then moved slowly toward Malaya and her mother. Malaya thought nothing of the first steps, except how nice it was the way the tapping of her heels against the floor seemed to punctuate the soft rub of the shimmery pantyhose: *gzhhh-TPP, gzhhh-TPP*. But within seconds Malaya could smell the woman's perfume in her face and found herself staring directly at the silver buckle on her purple suede belt.

Fear frothed up in Malaya's chest as the synthetic cherry stink of Ms. Adelaide's uncapped marker prickled the insides of her nostrils. She would lie, she decided. She would disclose a passion for yogurt, welcome and unusual in a girl of eight. Her face puffed with earnestness, she would tell the woman that she was centered, committed, and in control; that she'd take fat-free frozen yogurt over double-chocolate cookie dough ice cream any day. She would make her mother proud and make this lean purple creature go back and check her scale—those red numbers could *not* be right. This girl could not weigh one hundred and thirty two pounds, committed as she was. Malaya parted her lips and sucked in her stomach, prepared to declare her fidelity to the program.

Ms. Adelaide's mouth was plump and her red lipstick looked soft as jelly as it slid over her lip line into her deep brown skin. She tugged at the empty chair between Malaya and her mother, gently easing it from between the Clondon women's hips.

"I'm sorry, baby. Did you want to say something?"

Malaya paused, wondering if her lies were worth telling, now that it was clear she wasn't being asked to give up more than an empty chair. She shook her head no.

Professor Clondon looked at Malaya over the empty space where the chair had been and gave Ms. Adelaide a stiff half-smile. Malaya knew this smile. It was the smalltalk of her mother's facial lexicon, used to assert her presence and to make vague reference to Malaya, as if to say "Yes, that's my daughter." Ms. Adelaide smiled back.

"Well, everyone is so shy this morning!" She pushed the chair to the center of the room and glided into it like a goose into a familiar pond.

"So I'll tell you all first. My trigger food was corn with butter. Anytime there was corn around, I knew I would not be able to control myself. I used to be a corn *junkie*!" A few ladies along the wall chuckled. "And I don't mean just a little pat. I'm talking about *butter*, okay?"

At this, Ms. Adelaide changed shape before Malaya's eyes. She uncrossed her legs, hunched over, filled her cheeks with air and made smacking noises as she ran her fingers back and forth in front of her mouth, mimicking a wet and unsightly battle with an ear of corn on the cob. The room roared. Fat ladies shifted massive thighs in their chairs. Thick ladies clapped their hands and crashed against each other like waves.

"And let me tell you something." Ms. Adelaide leaned forward, pointing a finger at the group in a gesture of sistagirl confidence "I *know* I'm not the only one."

The whole room laughed again, and one rotund woman in the middle of the metal chair sea leaned her head back and opened her mouth so wide that Malaya thought she might freeze in that pose, turn to stone, and begin to spout water like a fish in a fountain. Then the meeting leader returned to herself, just like that— left leg draped over right, shoulders straight, manicured hands with their red-tipped nails resting so coolly on her lap one might never know she had briefly turned into a natural disaster just moments before.

"Well," the rotund woman said from the fourth or fifth row. "I do have a weakness for pasta."

"I heard that!" someone shouted. "What kind?"

And they were off, talking about food. Malaya didn't listen, except when Professor Clondon murmured in testimony when the women named foods Malaya knew she liked, like stewed oxtails and pistachio ice cream. As words began to appear on the easel's blank page, Malaya imagined each food rising from a plate before the woman who'd claimed it as her "trigger." Pieces of lasagna and tall Styrofoam-cupped milkshakes with cartoon eyes and gloved hands cuffed these women to their chairs in Malaya's imagination, dancing and singing devilishly as they leapt onto their plates. The women, helpless victims, dragged themselves sadly to these meetings each week, their only hope.

Quietly, in her mind, Malaya considered what this "trigger" food might be for her. But each food she thought of suddenly lost its appeal in the company of these women who seemed to feel guilty for putting too much gravy on their grits. She did not want to think about the French fries. She planned to eat them and to enjoy them as soon as she could leave her mother's sight. She would not ruin that moment by thinking of it now.

Instead, she reached down, lifted her legs onto her seat by the laces of her She-Ra sneakers, crossed her ankles as best she could, and thought of the fifth-grader Daundre Harris—her only good reason for trying to stay on-program at all. Each week as she waited for the numbers on the digital scale to stop climbing beneath her, she thought of Daundre and how much closer she might be to becoming Amandra Wilson, his pretty, skinny girlfriend, who had skin the color of a glazed doughnut and long hair that curled like Lo-Mein. Malaya had lost two pounds a year ago, when the family had just moved to Harlem. She was in the second grade then, and had beamed all week, sure that it was the beginning of a new life for her. She told her best friends Shanice Guzmán and Rachel Greenstein, then marked it in her Hello Kitty diary, along with the statement that Daundre had noticed her weight loss and asked her to be his girl, which was a lie. She even gave her grandmother the good news in a letter she wrote and mailed to Philadelphia all by herself. She gained four pounds the following week, but the letter had already arrived.

"My daughter and I like pie," Professor Clondon said, dropping her hand into her lap once the phrase was out. Malaya felt a force field of eyes on her.

"I don't keep anything like that in the house, of course," she continued. "And when we go out I try not to order dessert. But sometimes, on weekends, I'll order an apple pie…" Malaya anticipated the fancy syllables she knew would come next: "Á la mode."

"I try not to eat all the filling," Professor Clondon continued. "My favorite part is the crust. My daughter likes the filling, though. So if I do have a craving, rather than deprive myself, you know, I always suggest we share." The room gave a wave of supportive *mmhms*. "But you know children. They want their own. I don't usually let her order anything, but once we've eaten that pie we're out of control. We're off-program for the rest of the weekend, sometimes the whole week."

Ms. Adelaide added "PIE" to the list, which had grown to cover the entire page, leaving only a tiny strip of space between "SALMON CAKES" and "PLANTAIN CHIPS" for the three letters of the Clondon women's apparent trigger. Malaya wished to liquefy and slide from her seat, find herself gone from the basement into that word, PIE, curled into the lower nook of the E as though it were a shaded ground below an apple tree. She wished for spots of sun to heat her sandaled feet as the leaves of her E tree rustled, and for the cool of an afternoon to raise goose bumps along her long, lean legs. In truth, Malaya was not so compelled by pie. She would eat the filling because it was there, and because it would be one of very few chances she'd have all week to indulge herself in plain view, right beside her mother.

What Professor Clondon did not know, what could not be written on Ms. Adelaide's board for lack of space and language, was that Malaya would have preferred an endless plate of potatoes over pie, without question. Mashed, salted, swaddled in gravy or butter or both and served in a bottomless mixing bowl—that was how Malaya wanted to eat. She rarely had the opportunity; even when her mother and father weren't there to watch her, Collette, the babysitter, usually was. Malaya found her ways, though, sneaking bags of cereal from the basement kitchen in the sleeve of her nightgown, gulping down her own light yogurt cups quickly and volunteering to dispose of full-fat lunch leftovers for her friends. And by now, at eight years old, Malaya had noticed in herself a tendency to choose quantity over quality—pools and pools of potatoes over a shared slice of fancy pie. She had not yet learned words like *abundance* or *profusion* or *glut*; the only word she could find to describe her trigger was MORE. Of all the woman in the room—thirty at least—only two seemed to share her passion: the loud woman who had broken the ice what now seemed like ages ago, and a smaller woman beside her mother, who raised a hand only inches above her shoulder and said quietly, "I have trouble with plain white rice."

After the meeting, the Clondon women took the long route to the Harlem Arts Academy, walking up Adam Clayton Powell Jr. Boulevard to climb Sugar Hill at 145th. It had rained while they were inside, and now wet air stuck to Malaya's face as she held her mother's hand, watching different kinds of women pass through the streets. The Kingdom Hall of Jehovah's Witnesses was just across Frederick Douglass Boulevard, and Malaya watched as three women in trench coats, umbrellas, and gigantic church hats emerged from the building and stepped into the crosswalk. The tallest hat caught Malaya's eye—it was bright purple, and its mesh veil climbed up from behind the woman's ear and swept clear across her forehead as though it wanted to pinch her chin. She studied the color, planning to paint the hat in art class later in the day, after she'd eaten the French fries at last.

"Malaya." Her mother squeezed her hand in the drizzle. "You see those women? Big as houses over there? I hope you don't ever get that big."

Malaya nodded, confused, and looked closer. It was true that each woman was shaped like a house, she supposed, when she looked at them in a certain way.

The first woman was tall and thick like the brownstones on the Clondons' block, and, looking closely, Malaya guessed the two shorter women could look like some kind of shed or shack, though she had to squint to see it.

"I won't," she said plainly.

It was sweetly obvious. Malaya would not become a house. She could not imagine how those women had gotten that way, and had not really thought before that moment that that might be a way to *become* at all. It seemed to her that either a person was born a house or she wasn't; Malaya wasn't.

"I hope you don't," Professor Clondon continued. "People like that are very unhealthy. They lead very unhappy lives, and they die young."

Malaya nodded again, emphatically this time. It angered her that her mother could doubt her on so sure an issue as this. She imagined her ears stuffed with cotton balls, blocking out her mother's voice, leaving room in her head only for thoughts of sweet things and French fries.

When they reached the Harlem Arts Academy, Professor Clondon stooped to give Malaya her $4 allowance and a kiss. Malaya smooched the air around her mother's cheek and promised to hold onto the money in case of an emergency. As Professor Clondon disappeared from sight, Malaya stuck the money in the pocket of her backpack.

Entering the dance hallway, she shuffled past the bread-stick legs of ballet and jazz dance students, toward the African Dance corner. Here, the girls wore black leotards that stretched over their flat torsos like spans of gift wrap over book covers, and red, yellow, and green printed *lapas* that hung merrily around their waists like garlands. She tried not to look too hard as she neared them. For Malaya, the *lapa* was the one secret pleasure of dance class. It was a glorious stretch of Kente-print cloth that covered the worst of her middle and, when pulled tight enough, held her stomach in and made a waist for her hips. She hated undressing in the hallway—hated the eyes on all parts of her body—but the thought of the fries and the feeling of the *lapa* helped to dull the sting.

She reached her corner wordlessly and turned toward the wall, squeezing herself into the fabric. Breathing in deep, she tugged at the straps of the bra she had stolen from her mother's bureau earlier that week, which still smelled like her mother's hair grease. By the time she turned around, the hallway was empty and the drums had begun to play.

Dance Studio One was a huge room with a wall full of mirrors and a floor so smooth that if you ran on it in pantyhose and stopped short, you could slide for miles. Some girls did come to class in pantyhose, and on the first day of class Malaya had been one of them. Unable to find real dance clothes in Malaya's size, Professor Clondon went instead to the Woolworth's after the meeting and brought back a black bathing suit in a women's size 12 and a pair of extra large panty hose in opaque black.

"Can't y'all read!" Mrs. Rhymes, the trunk-legged dance teacher screamed, holding a copy of the class description in he air. "'Footless Dancin Tights!' I don't want to see none of y'all in here in stockin's! This is about respeck!"

Malaya went home that afternoon crying, and by Thursday of the following week, Professor Clondon had brought home two pairs of extra large women's footless dance tights from who-knew-where.

Malaya stood in the back of the room and watched in the mirror while the other students gathered for warm-up period, bending and stretching just enough to avoid calling Mrs. Rhymes's attention while they giggled about which drummer they thought was cute and which one had messed up teeth. All of the girls were smaller that Malaya. The younger girls' tall, straight bodies made Malaya think of how ostriches must have looked before they grew their fluffy behinds. But the older girls had the kinds of bodies Malaya dreamed about, hips that curved and sloped with unreal symmetry, narrow legs that shone like wet licorice in their iridescent black tights. Though she was much wider than the oldest of those girls, the bra and *lapa* gave Malaya a taste of that body, a hint of what it might feel like to be only a little loose at the top, cinched tight in the middle, and round and full at the bottom. She parted her legs slightly, raised her left arm over her head, bent her torso to the side, and explored this curve in the mirror.

Soon, Mrs. Rhymes demonstrated the first step for the day, her heavy legs moving in a simple side-to-side march, her hips grabbing hold of the rhythm. The girls gathered in the corner of the room and watched, ready to repeat the step in pairs across the wood floor. While the other girls chatted and watched, Malaya listened to the chorus of drums and played games with the sounds in her head. She studied the steady *bum-bum-bap*! of the lowest drum, pulling it apart from the *shhka-shh-shh* of the *shakerays* and the *brrrap-dap-dap!* of the louder bass until she could hear each of them separately. Every few seconds, she glanced over at the dance floor to make sure she wasn't missing too much. The first few steps of the routine were usually manageable—it was only at the midpoint of the class that the steps got complicated. Feeling the curve of her hip with her hand, she watched Mrs. Rhymes's feet tap and fly across the bright wood, trusting that her own feet would do the same when her turn came. Then she returned to thinking about the drums, letting her mind drift into the music. She was standing in the middle of the floor with Mrs. Rhymes crouched down like a gargoyle in her face when she realized that, today, the twist to the step had come too soon.

"You! What's wrong with your body?" the teacher shouted, spreading her arms out wide. The two girls in front of Malaya were reaching into the air and pulling their elbows down in time with their feet in the step. Malaya glanced at the girl beside her, who was doing the same. Only Malaya had forgotten to raise her arms.

No response came to Malaya's mind, other than, *Nothing, what's wrong with your face?* which, of course, she couldn't say. Her cheeks felt hot and her eyes began to sting.

"The step is *ba-ba- ba-ba da-DA!*" The woman pounded the floor with her heels, reaching at the ceiling with her arms and neck, grabbing what could have been a coconut from the air and tucking it down toward her stomach in time with the beat.

"You got to be in your body, girl! Move your arms! Your feet!"

But Malaya had been moving her body. She had not noticed the addition of arms to the step, that was true. And her footwork may not have been as quick or as pretty as the others', but still, she felt she had moved. The tears came down hot now.

"You got to learn to be in that body of yours!" Mrs. Rhymes said again. She shot her hand out and pinched Malaya hard on her side where her *lapa* was knotted. Then she looked past Malaya at the rest of the class. "You have to disciplint yo mind, ladies! This is about respeck!"

Malaya felt the pinch still and deep in her side, even as the woman walked away. She imagined "disciplint" as a vise on her head, a metal sheet clamped and soldered over her mouth and eyes. The word made her think of pain worse than too-tight pantyhose and Ms. Adelaide's marker, worse than a life spent longing for French fries, or for a Friday night with her father that would never come. She and her dance partner repeated the step, the other girl moving with fresh vigor, Malaya floating through the movements without the vaguest commitment to the dance or the drums. Even the hope of salt-showered fries slunk silently from her mind. She spent the rest of the class daydreaming about sleep, wishing for a world in which she could close her eyes and wake up long and lean and limber, or a life in which she could actually crawl quiet and alone into the bottom nook of a letter E, curl up, read a book, eat an apple.

Malaya still felt the dance teacher's pinch when she got to the cafeteria after class. She felt it as she ordered her French fries, her voice unsure and trembling. The memory of it soured in her mouth as she ate the fries, making them taste like chalk. The pinch was with her all the way through painting class, through homework help, through dinner back at home. She felt it when she crept into the kitchen in the late hours of the night to grab Friday's leftover Chinese food containers and sneak them up to her room, covered by the folds of her nightgown.

Sitting alone in her room with the leftovers in her lap, Malaya turned off her lamp and spooned heaps of hard rice and cold, congealed gravy into her mouth, waiting for the pinch to leave her. She fed herself to the sounds of the street: the laughter, the sirens, the squeaking of sneakers in late-night games of double-dutch and streetball. She ate until her stomach felt good, and then until it hurt, and then until it felt like it wasn't there at all.

There was a feeling Malaya Clondon imagined, a fantasy that grew in her around that time and stayed with her for years after. She imagined the feeling of sliding from good dreams, glad to be in real life. She thought of waking one day—and the next day, and the next—not sad and slow and praying to crawl back up into sleep, but quickly—with a lightness and a spring. She had tasted this feeling in the pre-dawn hours before trips to the roller coaster park, or during the first short breaths of Christmas day. On those days, she would leap out of her dreams like a splash of water from a boiling pot, ready for what the day might become. But most mornings, like this one, Malaya lay stiffly in bed, wishing for the sun to disappear. Done with reality, she wished to be swallowed into her dreams.

To be nice, she thought, the spoon heavy in her

hand, she might consider visiting this life she'd left. She might float out of her dream, back over these steps for a while, might hover above the meetings and watch calmly as the dance teacher pinched hard seconds into her flesh. In a show of grace and generosity, Malaya might reach down from her elsewhere, and listen from an easy distance to her mother's voice on the stairs, crackling its first chords of the day:

"Malaya, get in the shower! You have to wake up!"

She would say "No," politely but clearly. Malaya would not stay.

Sererie

When disappeared girls are lucky, they go to other places and hook their husbands' names to theirs like snake cords to clothing sacks. Then they send messages back home, telling us who they are now. Before today, when I was a child, I thought this was what happened to my sister, Azmera. I thought she disappeared to New York and became Azmera Mitslal, a man's wife, a woman, with a face and a life as new as a baby's. But Azmera was not lucky. This is what I am learning now.

Before today, my Abeselome would laugh when I talked about my sister's extra name. "There must be Azmeras flitting in the New York air like flies," he would say, cutting his eyes and smiling. "Even more than Addis Ababa. She has to let them know which Azmera she is, so they do not think she is one of the *other* Azmeras. The singing star Azmera, the woman doctor Azmera. The president." He would throw his head back and let his teeth spread over his face like the pale stone walls of the churches behind our compound. I would smile and tell him his walls were crumbling, that his teeth would fall like the ruins if he continued to make jokes on my sister. Azmera is as pretty as a singer, I would tell him, and as smart as a president. Her face is slick like the inside of a bee's hive and her eyes are quick and sharp. But he would just laugh deeper, his face opening wide like a bathing pool, until I could only jump in and laugh with him.

This was our *qene*, our back-and-forth talk. We kicked words across the air like rocks in a boys' game, stashed the meanings in each other like playing hide-and-seek. Abeselome's qene has always been good; he is sixteen, has been growing up and learning things two years longer than me. He goes to the school and gathers new words, a new story-full every week. Then he comes home and kicks the words to me. I stop them with my eyes, turn them around in my head, kick them back. My qene is good, he tells me, and I know. My qene is from my family; they put it in my name: Meraffe, chapter. My qene goes for days and days.

Back when we were children, when Azmera was still here, she joined in the qene. So did Genet, who is Azmera's best friend and Abeselome's sister, and now my sister, too. The four of us would play language games, passing words between us from the time the sun spilled white on the ruins till our mothers called us all home to eat. Now that we are grown and Azmera is gone—and my parents gone too—Genet and I keep the qene up when Abeselome is at the school. We sit with Persinna, Genet and Abeselome's mother, pulling dead roots from the ground and saying they look like feet or ghosts or the mark that used to live between my mother's eyes. We spice the sebbi for dinner and say it smells like the dirt did before the drought, when rain seemed always in the air, when we did not have to close our eyes and breathe deep to remember moisture in our mouths. When our talk gets sad, going back to the days of Azmera, Genet touches my face and smiles at me. Genet loves Azmera, feels as dry without her as I do. "They are like us when we were girls," our mothers used to say, their laughter mixing like the string chords of a lyre. "Friendship is more than friendship to them." So when Azmera slips into our talk, I rub my cheek against Genet's palm and we turn our qene quickly back to battle-play, pulling good words from each other's lips and sticking them to the things around us, seeing who can draw the tighter wince, the thicker laugh.

Through our laughter, I try to forget the story of Azmera's disappearance. I try instead to hold on to Genet, to keep her from leaving, too. Genet's body is like Azmera's was when she was here. It is thin and long and moves quick along the ground, like a shadow after dinnertime. She brushes through our compound, behind the griddles, under the mats, cleaning messes in the kitchen, clearing junk from the road, as though if she stood too still in the light, she would be in someone's way. Azmera was the same, though it seemed to me then that Genet was just a breath quicker, her qene tumbling just a half-step ahead.

Before Azmera disappeared, she and Genet were always rushing, rushing to take care of things—of Abeselome, of me, of the cats and cows that died because it refused to rain. When the two of them were not rushing, they were gone—I didn't know to where. I knew only that it felt like a holiday when they came back, when they slowed and stilled and paused for me. They were the grown ones, the tall, pretty ones who talked with their mouths turned down like women. I remember looking at them, wanting always to join them in their secret places, to be like them in a friendship like theirs when I got to be their age. Genet was seventeen then, and Azmera, when we knew her, was seventeen too. But that was a year ago; I do not know what Azmera is now, how much older she has grown.

Now our qene is what keeps me and Genet up, keeps our spirits holding our faces in the right way. Abeselome keeps us smiling, too, helps us not to think about what we have lost. Genet and Abeselome learned the trick a long time ago, they say, when their father died in the usual way, air blowing through his stomach like a sandstorm through the ruins, his body laid out like a mat for the mosquito disease. That's when they started to distract themselves with qene, making words into puzzles so that any spare moment could become a game. My mother was generous and loved Persinna, and there had been food and rain and a pinch of money then, so she asked my father to make a house for Persinna in our compound after their father died. "Your man is a good one," Persinna would say to my mother when we were all together. "He is kind, and he is here." My father would smile and kiss my mother's head, and Persinna would look down at Abeselome to be sure he was watching, which he always was.

Now Abeselome brings me and Genet words from the school and we gobble them quickly into our word games, sticking them to our names and to Azmera's to see what meanings we can make. Abeselome is *resplendent*, we say, bright and happy like a girl's ashenda dance. Azmera's jokes are *shrewd*, we say, tight as a head full of freshly-done braids. We like this game; it makes us feel closer to Azmera, and also to my parents and to their father, who put good qene in our names. Our families named us in Amharic—not Tigre, not Tigrinya—because our parents wanted good fortune for us when we became old. Amharic is not the language of power, our mothers would say, but it is a first sound. Persinna reminds me of this when I miss Azmera and our life. "Your parents gave you your futures," she says. "As long as you both are living, they can't be gone."

I did not think so much of names or futures or how the world came to be until Azmera disappeared. Before, when I was a girl, I only listened to church talk and bible stories like they were pretty songs. I already knew my favorite version of how people were made. No magic babies, no big man bringing things in twos, in twos, no room for odd matches. I thought only of Gebre Memfis Qudus, my favorite hero from the saint stories.

When I hear this story, I see Gebre Memfis wrapped in a gabbi as wide as a canyon and as white as a new chick's hair. The cloth is so thick that you cannot tell if Gebre Memfis is a man or a woman or a baby or an ox; you know only that he is kind because you can feel his smile. In my version of the story, Gebre Memfis is walking through the place where our compound is, only it is more years ago than there are hairs on my head. The dirt is always wet, the sky always hangs low with rain. Gebre Memfis is walking and singing his song, and he sees a bird on the ground that is so dry it is going to die. Gebre Memfis is good, and so he cries for the bird. The bird is good too, and smart. It feels Gebre Memfis' sadness, and so it opens its mouth to give Gebre Memfis soft qene. Then the tears splash into the bird's beak and the bird is not dry any more. It drinks from Gebre Memfis and is born, and flies away. It is so happy about what it has learned that it tells its bird family, and they are so happy they chirp and sing and make a world.

I did not think any more of how things came to be until now, now when my parents are dead and my sister is gone and the only things I have are Abeselome here in my bed with me and Genet singing a one-string song to the pots outside. Now, with Abeselome with me, I am thinking of my sister, of the man who dropped on top of her like a dead hawk and pounded her into nothing, made her disappear. I think of this and I try to make sense of what is happening right now.

This is the story Azmera told me: one afternoon, while our parents were out and I was with Abeselome and Genet was patching clothes in her mother's house, Azmera opened the door for Akrham, the big-breasted woman who lives in the compound across the road. Azmera was tired and busy, working in the kitchen, but Akrham said she needed spice for her dinner. Akrham was always nice, with big sad eyes like an old cow's. Azmera and I liked to look at her when she came over to gossip with our mother, liked to watch her eyelashes sweep her cheeks when she laughed. And so, Azmera told me, she let the woman in, gave her the spice, talked about the dry air and the neighbors while she made teheni flour for our mother to store away.

Azmera asked Akrham about her family, about her brother, Biserat, who had just come back from two

years in Mekele, where he went to weave cloth.
Akrham's father was gone, like Genet's and
Abeselome's, and people talked badly about Biserat
for leaving his mother and his sister to farm alone.
Sometimes Azmera would join in the talk, whispering
with Genet as they washed the plates at night: *what
kind of person would leave his people broke like that?
What kind of man?* But Azmera was generous like our
mother. She did not want Akrham to feel bad. When
Akrham came for the spice, she asked about Biserat
with a smile, I know, and with only a speck of
mischief stuck between her teeth. She offered Akrham
some sips of beer and told her she had dreamed Biserat
would do great things for his family, which was a lie.
When the beer was done and the conversation had
foamed away, Azmera went back to cooking and told
Akrham she could let herself out.

I was in the shrubs with Abeselome, but I can see
it like I was a grain of wheat dust on the floor: Akrham
leaves and Azmera holds the bowl, stirs the barley,
adds the water. She lights a fire under the uton stove,
getting ready to roll the mix into dough. But the rolling
does not come, and instead comes the man, Biserat,
without a knock, or a word, or the quick click of the
door latch undone. "How could she let him in like
that?" Azmera says to me later, looking in my
direction but talking to the air. "Did she know what he
would do?" But there he is, Biserat, talking bad qene
to my sister, pinching at her legs like dough, then
pushing into her as though he is making a pot in her
stomach. He tells her he will marry her, make a family
with her. He talks wildly about a dowry, says that
marrying her will make him a man. He says he will

protect her, will tell no one what she's done. "Have I done something?" She says later, to the air. She says "I swear, I told him no." I don't know what to say, so I touch her hand. I wasn't there, but I see it still: Azmera kneeling in our mother's kitchen, her fingers gripping the stove our mother built, the man making Azmera into his own seething griddle.

When I come home, Azmera is rolled up like an onion on the kitchen floor. She tells me the story and she cries. With her eyebrows stitched tight across her face, she says "Don't tell Genet." I want to ask her why not, but when I open my mouth she stops me with her eyes and I know I am not supposed to understand. Then she tells me not to tell our parents, either, says that if I tell them, they will die.

This is the part of the story I remember when Abeselome and me get in the bed together. Before today I did not understand why a man would drop himself on my sister, or why knowing this would make my parents die. I knew other things, things about how to mold clay and bend metal for a stove, how to listen to the air for rain, how to tell whether a woman is trustworthy by the way she holds her neck. I knew which names were for power and which were for thankless work. But I did not know why a man would do that to my sister, or why it would make my family disappear.

When I think of this, with Abeselome here with me, I am scared. I worry that I will curl into an onion and roll away. I smell his breath and I wonder if it smells like Biserat's, if what happened to Azmera is what is happening to me.

After the man dropped himself on Azmera, her face became flat and empty as a plastic bag. She began to float around the kitchen, sweeping so limply that, between her and the broom handle, I was not sure who was holding who. Every morning, as soon as our parents had left for the day, she would rush out of the compound and open her mouth to vomit, spilling the last day's food into the shrubs. When I asked her what was wrong, she would look past my head and say, "I'm fine." But when Genet or our parents came around, she tried to make herself tall and bright, pretending that everything was better than fine. She would touch Genet's face and smile, her mouth pink and gummy. Then they would walk together, out of the compound, down the road to wherever they went, touching, laughing. But as soon as Genet had gone home, Azmera would seem weaker than before, the light slipping from her face like a puddle into sand.

She faded further and further with each week that passed, each story Abeselome brought home. Six stories after Biserat hurt her, Azmera told me about a girl she once heard Genet mention. The girl lived in a compound near the ruins in Slehleka, an hour's walk away. Genet said the girl got sick after a man dropped on her. She said the girl went first to the Family Guidance clinic in Mekele, where she talked with a woman whose face was white and cracked like a compound's outer wall, and whose hair was yellow and flat. She had only seen women who looked like that on television, and once in a traveller van in Addis Ababa. She didn't have a good feeling about people like that, but her problem was getting too big for her to manage alone, so she talked to the Family Guidance woman anyway. The woman showed her a machine that would suck the problem away, like poison from a snake bite, the girl had said. But the woman was rude and talked to her like a child, she said, and the look of metal machine scared her. And so she went instead to Kassa, the hakym, who tells people what to eat when they are sick and fixes them when their bodies are broken. Azmera felt that she should go to Kassa, too, that he would know what to do. *Do about what?* I wanted to ask. But her lips were braided tightly together and I knew she did not want to answer questions.

I never liked Kassa, and I hate him now. Before I went with Azmera, I had visited him only once, when our father started coughing so hard I thought a rabbit tail was stuck in his throat. Kassa gave my father a tea to drink every day and said he would be like new in only ten days—ten times faster, he said, than if he had gone to the clinic in Mekele. He gave a jagged smile that looked like the tread of a tractor wheel and leaned back in his chair. I did not like how proud he seemed, how sure of his own power. My father said the tea tasted terrible, like birds' leavings. In the end, the mosquito disease took him anyway. He died with the taste of bird shit in his mouth.

I disliked Kassa from then on, but this was Azmera, my older sister, who only told me no when saying yes would harm me. And so, when she asked me to go with her, I pressed her fingers together in mine to slow her shaking, and we walked down the road, past the children and the dogs, past the brittle fields, to Kassa's house.

When we got there, Azmera broke off parts of the story for him like chips from a block of salt. I did not understand then why she told it that way, only in parts. She said nothing about the falling man or what he had done to her. She said only that she was not feeling well, that she had had a very bad headache for six weeks now—the worst kind of headache a girl could have, she said—and she needed a tea to make it go away. Kassa gave Azmera his bent-up smile and a package of a frilly herb that he called abewela.

"It's not tea you need," he said, lighting a fire under a pot of water. "It's steam." He told her to cut the root of the abewela and heat it over a tall fire until the steam made her teeth draw tight. Then he told her to take her pants down and squat over the fire as though she were peeing in the shrubs. He held his gabbi to his legs and bent over the pot to show her what he meant.

"Ten minutes," he said, "and it will clean the problem away." Then he clapped his hands together as though putting a final letter on a sentence he did not want to hear. Azmera gave him a fistful of birr, enough to buy a tower of books, I thought, and we left. I don't know where she got the money from. Some things I am glad I don't understand, and this is one.

One week later, our mother went to Mekele to sell our weakest cow. I was sad about it, but our mother put her hand on my head and told me not to worry. "She is old and thirsty and tired of working," she said. "Someone can eat her. She won't mind."

Once she had left, Azmera put a pot on the fire and followed Kassa's instructions. When the steam hit between her legs, her breath made a sound like a busted tire and her head rolled back so quickly I worried it would snap. When she brought her head forward again, her cheeks were sliding in water, her face curled around itself like a handful of metal scraps. She stood there for ten minutes, like Kassa told her, her shoulders jerking quickly back and forth. I remember this moment clearly now: soon I am crying too, begging her to move from the fire. But she digs her toes into the floor and closes her eyes to me.

Only now, touching Abeselome, do I recognize the smell that soaked from Azmera into the floor that day. I smell Abeselome, notice how his sweat is different from mine—his sour and sharp like gasoline, mine mild and gritty like meal. As he moves over me I notice our smells mixing, making something new. Now I understand what was in Azmera's blood, why it was thick as red lentils left too long on the fire, why she had me bury the cleaning rags deep in the dirt far outside the compound. Why I can still smell her when I walk by that spot, my favorite spot now that she's gone.

Now I recognize the smell, but I still wonder why this happens, why my body is doing this, why Azmera's body did what it did, how Abeselome's body can do the things it is doing right now. Now I understand that there are too many stories I have not heard, too many things I do not know, more things than there are names for. Or, if there are names, I don't know them either.

Three weeks after we visited Kassa, Azmera came to tell me that the abewela steam was not enough. She said this with her voice slung so low to the ground that I imagined it growing white and heavy with clay dirt. When our mother went to visit Persinna

109

that afternoon, we darted through the house like moths, looking for a solution to Azmera's problem, the problem that had no name.

Eventually I had the idea to look under our mother's mat for the sack where she kept her private things. This sack, for me, held all adulthood's secrets. It was my own private joy, before, to sneak to the mat when no one was watching, pick up the sack and run my fingers through its contents: my mother's money, my grandmother's chain necklace, the little wire dolls Azmera and I used to make, back when we were girls. The sack was the color of an overripe plum, wrapped in a gold braid that had always been old, had always been shedding shimmering strings like a gold cat's tail, promising that there could be worlds of treasure inside of any small thing. I had not looked in the sack in a while, but I was sure that Azmera's answer was bound up beneath that rope.

When we opened the sack and let the loose strings flutter to the floor, we found the dolls, and the birr, and the necklace. There was also a silent, silver-colored watch that Azmera and our mother had once found on the side of the road one day, along with a few strange coins. There were pages of writing I could not read, pieces of broken jewelry I had never seen, and a package of dried sererie leaf.

I recognized the sererie right away; Abeselome and I had had good qene about its shape. The leaves reach out and up at first, then bend over themselves, their tips grazing their roots like a bouquet of closing hands. Our mother used to grow this plant in a small plot at the edge of our part of the farm. I did not know what the plant was for, but I knew that it was important, because she pulled its roots every month; every four stories the hands would disappear. Sometimes, too, I saw her pull the sererie between months and share them with other women who lived nearby. When I asked her what it was, she said, "It helps women keep families small enough to feed." Then she sent me a sharp look and said, "But you're not a woman, so questions like that are not for you. Go and spice the sebbi. Or if you want, go play."

I didn't know what she meant then—I only knew to stop asking. But later, from the scraps of the story fluttering around me, I started to put things together. If this was a problem women had, perhaps we needed help from a woman. We couldn't talk to our mother— that was clear. And Azmera wouldn't even let Genet know, let alone Persinna. We sifted back through all our names and stories and thought of the Family Guidance woman again. Mekele was three hours away, across a patchwork of roads, busses, and footpaths. We would need a day to ourselves to get there and back.

But a whole day seemed an impossible luxury. Looking at the dried sererie, its leaves curled under the frayed gold rope, I thought maybe it could help us. I didn't know yet what it was, but I knew it was important to our mother, and to other women, and I knew it was almost gone. We had heard our mother talk about making the trip to Mekele to buy seeds so she could plant more, but with the pitiful harvests and the cost of the trip, we couldn't know if she would really go, or when. Though there wasn't enough sererie for all the women anymore, there seemed to be just enough for her, for now. And that was too much for us if we needed her to give us a day alone.

So, holding the shriveled plant together, Azmera and I began to bake a plan. We would help the sererie disappear, we said. Sererie was strong—we knew we could not eat it or we'd get sick. We did not know how, and we did not want to know. Instead, we decided, we would grind it up and feed it to Akrham's cows. We would fold the leaves into squares and hide them under our mats, in our shoes. We would stuff it in the pockets of our pants and carry it out to the edge of the compound to bury with the red-soaked rags. Then, when our mother went looking for the plant, two or three weeks later, we would open our eyes as wide as the camels' and say we didn't know, maybe Biserat stole it. We would offer to go to the market to buy the seeds for her, and then we would go to the Family Guidance Clinic, where they fixed problems like ours, whatever that might have been.

We gathered the plant, prepared our plans. But Abeselome's stories came and the weeks passed and our mother did not ask about the sererie. She and my father began to look as dry as the dirt. They began to wilt like the plants and thin like the cows and grew quiet as the stranger's old tickless watch.

My Abeselome had brought twelve new stories home by the time I opened my mouth to Genet. I told her early one morning, while Azmera was still asleep and Abeselome was on his way to the school. Our mothers were out in the field, weeding for the harvest, laughing about the neighbors, wishing for rain, and our father was far away, plowing at the field's horizon. I looked at Genet's pretty cheeks, and I thought of Azmera, how she was draining to nothing, soaking like the blood smell into her mat. And so I opened my mouth.

I told Genet about everything—about the hakym and the steam bath and what Biserat did. Genet's eyes went flat while I talked, then they welled up and I thought she would cry. But when I told her about the sererie, her face drew sharp as a bele pear thorn.

"Stupid," she said. "Sererie is what she needs."

When we woke Azmera up, she knew right away that I had told her secret. While Genet cried and yelled over her, Azmera looked at me, her eyes whittled to a point. But soon, Genet was done yelling. She pulled Azmera from the mat, kissed her face and held her shoulders still. "Get the sererie," she told me. And Genet was wise and I knew nothing, so I picked up the sheet from my mat and went all through the compound and out to the shrubs collecting the sererie we had hid, retracing my steps like hide-and-seek in reverse.

When I came back to the compound, Genet and Azmera were in Persinna's house, sitting on Genet's mat with a big meat knife, an empty water bottle, and the metal stick from an umbrella. A pot of water was boiling on the stove, and Azmera was crumpled like an old shirt, part of her draped on Genet's shoulder, the rest of her trailing into the floor. Genet motioned for me to pass her my folded sheet, but I hesitated.

"What are we going to do now?" I asked. "What if someone comes?"

Genet looked at me, annoyed again, and told me our mothers would be weeding all day, and that if Persinna did come home she would not be angry or tell our parents. "Anyway," she said, "we have to do something. This is the best thing we can do."

With her legs curved and opened wide, Azmera lay down on the mat. She held her breath while Genet gathered the sererie and broke the umbrella stick to a finger length. She pierced the cap of the bottle with the knife and stuck the metal tube in. Then she chopped the leaves until they lay in soft mounds on the floor like piles of sheep's hair, and put them in the water and let them boil. "Hold her hand," she told me, and I did, remembering how it felt when we walked to Kassa's house. Her hand was warm then, and it buzzed inside of mine. But now it was still and soft and hot and cool at once, almost unfamiliar.

Genet poured the water into the bottle, blowing lightly on the rim. "It has to be hot," she said to Azmera. "I'm sorry." When the bottle was full, she ran the tips of her fingers along Azmera's legs as though she were tracing a favorite route on a map. Then she pressed down on Azmera's knee, gudied the umbrella stick past her hips, and squeezed the bottle. She talked sweet qene the whole time, telling Azmera how she was the prettiest girl in the world, how we all loved her as much as we loved days and songs, how soon she would be better and soon there would be rain and soon everything really would be better than fine. When Genet squeezed the bottle again, Azmera drew a deep breath, as though she were trying to suck in all the room's air through the little hole of her mouth. Then Genet climbed gently over her and curled up, like for sleep. She pushed her hands hard three times below Azmera's belly button, then waited, and pushed and pushed again. Each time, Azmera's mouth popped open, and I thought she would scream, but Genet reached up and laid her palm on her lips so that no sound came out.

When it was over, Genet packed Azmera's legs with sheets and old cloth and gave her a wide, dark gabbi to cover the bulk. While I cleaned the floor, Genet touched Azmera's face and kissed her shoulders and laced trails of butter under her braids. Azmera leaked and shook while Genet dressed her, breathing heavily over Genet's arms, never looking at me. When the cleaning was done and it was time for Azmera and me to go back to our compound, Azmera made herself tall and straight again, flattening her face and her eyes, squaring her shoulders, training her breath. Genet touched Azmera's shoulder and Azmera looked at her for two seconds' ticks, her eyes cloudy with words, her mouth quiet as dust. Then she turned out of the room and walked to our compound, not even checking to see if I was behind her.

Two days later, Azmera was gone. First to Mekele, where she lived a life I do not know about, and then to New York, where she is the wife of a man named Mitslal, a two-name woman, with another life I do not know. When I ask Persinna to tell me the chapters of Azmera's disappearance—the parts of the story that nobody has told me—she says she doesn't know either, but I'm not sure if I believe her. Still, I am afraid to ask more questions, afraid of what I don't know, which, I am learning, is so, so much.

Now, with Azmera gone, Genet tells me that she has been afraid, too. She tells me she was afraid on the day of the sererie. She worried that Abeselome would come home early from the school, that my father would stop in for a clean sweat rag, or that one of our mothers would come looking for us, to see how far we had come with dinner. Then she tells me she has lived a long time with fears like those, fears of being discovered doing what she was not supposed to do. She says those fears are old for her now, as old as her name, so old that she has learned not to think about them, just to live. She is used to hiding, she says, and Azmera was too. When she tells me this she looks like Azmera did while she was disappearing—like she is hiding a story in her mouth, something important that she will never say.

Now, with Abeselome touching my face and my chest, talking sweet qene, making me feel good, this is when I start to understand. This is when I see why Azmera did not want Genet to know the story, why she felt it might kill her. This when I see that Azmera could not stay here, that she could not stay Azmera. This is when I know that it was not luck that sent her over the ocean and strapped her down to a man and his name. This is when I know that it was love.

Everyone says that our parents died in the usual way, of the mosquito disease, going narrow as cats, their faces fading to the color of millet. Some tell the story that they missed my sister, and were ashamed to have her run to the city and across the ocean for no reason with a man they never met. Persinna says they did not die at all, that they are still here, swimming inside of me, in my spirit, in my blood. I wonder if they are waiting to come out again.

Genet says she did not tell Persinna about the sererie, but I'm not sure. When I talk to Persinna now, I see her avoiding words, swerving her tongue around them like bad pepper seeds in a stew. I don't know why she will not tell me. She looks at me and I think she knows what happened, that she told my parents about Biserat, and that they could not take it. I worry that, by opening my mouth to Genet, I made my parents die.

I think about all this now with Abeselome here with me, his fingers sliding over my hips like Genet's fingers, his mouth spreading over my chest like Genet did. I smell the smells and feel the push and I am glad that I do not want to swallow everyone's air like Azmera did. That what I am feeling is not pain. I look at Abeselome, see his lips curve up timidly, and I think that he is not like Kassa, not like Biserat. With him, I almost always smile, and my breath is easy and calm. But as he touches me he makes a grunting noise, and I wonder if these are the noises Biserat made. He sees my confusion and asks if we should go outside, do something else, but I do not know what to say. I look past him at the ceiling like Azmera and say, "I'm fine."

He tickles me, runs his fingers along my neck and wrists, blows on my skin as though I were a flute. I ask my skin to sing for him, but it is quiet. I try to think of good things, of Azmera's face and deep, slow voice, the way she looked with Genet lacing butter along the shoreline of her braids. But I can't think of these things. All I can think of is the smell of my sister drunk into the floor, the long, low sound of her last real breath, the lonely walk back from Persinna's home to ours, a walk that did not ever really end.

It has been only a year since she disappeared but it feels to me like so much time—a whole ocean of chapters, a whole skyfull of stories. It is only now that I feel I have learned them—the stories of Azmera, of

Genet's friend from Slehleka, of who-knows-how-many-else, whose bodies and choices were taken, so all they could do was find a way to leave. It is only right now, with Abeselome touching me, and me touching back, that I know what their stories are about. And now, understanding, I feel that I am grown.

While Abeselome blows sweet breath on my forehead I try to think of Gebre Memfis. But that is a different kind of story, I know now. A made-up tale like any other, pretty and silly as a holiday song. What happened to Azmera—*that* is how things are, how people come to be.

Abeselome talks his best qene, words thick and sweet dripping over me, but I am dry. I try to smile, to kick words back, but my lips are pinned together and my mind is blank. I look up at the ceiling, down at the floor, at Abeselome. He kisses my nose, his eyes two heavy clouds sagging with rain, but still I am afraid. I will not open like the dry bird's beak. My fingers, my lips, my limbs are folded over like the sererie, and I am closed.

A Magic of Bags

When Ilana Randolph left her house that Saturday night, the only people outside were on their way. It was April, and past midnight, and the air was black and wet as a glass of diet cola. The dealers, the addicts, the stoop ladies—everyone who usually populated the block was elsewhere now. The women of the Harlem Grange Homeowners' Council were in their brownstones, packing lunches, rinsing their pantyhose, preparing for the next day's climb. Only a handful of shadows moved under the streetlight as Ilana pushed through the blocks toward Convent Avenue, a garbage bag full of babies in tow.

Everyone knew Ilana was unusual, even before the babies. She couldn't have denied it if she'd wanted to—which she didn't. It wasn't just that she was wide as a refrigerator and always wore purple and orange extensions in her hair, or that she painted her nails wacky colors like black and neon green—though the Grange Women were none too impressed by any of that either. But Ilana's difference went deeper. Most of the Grange's young people spent their free time hopping subway turnstiles on the way home from their private schools, smoking loosies in Riverside Park in feeble defiance of authority, plotting futures with one-another, most of which ended with masters' degrees from MIT and expensive wedding receptions in opulent hotels downtown. Ilana, on the other hand, spent her time alone, meditating on a single idea: verticality. Not in the dull, sentimental, *lift-as-you-climb, movin'-on-up* kind of sense, though she felt that was important in a historical way. But Ilana was interested in the more meaningful sense of up and down movement: the apparent versus the subterranean, how things arranged themselves on the surface versus what really held them together the core.

She pondered this notion constantly, doodling diagrams of plants' roots and soil strata in her Spanish notebooks, writing songs about nectarine pits, subway tunnels and the penny-studded floors of fountains whenever she got the chance. While everyone around her strived desperately or attractiveness, Ilana was sure the body must have some better use. She was ever on a quest to get under the skin of things—and to mess with them. Not in a bad way. Just in a way that proved she was there.

The Grange Women, Ilana knew, would attribute her strangeness to her father's death from bone cancer, a year before the babies. But Ilana's penchant for troublemaking began much longer ago than that. Once, when she was fourteen, she won $100 for taking first place in a local High School Heroes essay contest, and it was when she went to the check cashing place on Edgecombe with the prize check that she first discovered her magic. When she entered, the man behind the counter greeted her by exclaiming "Hey, big girl—I like those baby-bouncin' hips!" with a gin-soaked but not insincere smile. Deeply insulted but unsure what to say, Ilana stared at the man, focusing hard, until she thought she could feel her gaze buzzing just below the gray hair on his left arm. She wanted to make him itch. It was a good feeling, and so she focused harder, training her eyes on his arm as she handed over her check and ID. Staring imperceptibly for all those minutes wasn't easy, but it was gratifying—many times, she felt the need to blink, but she rallied and instead intensified her gaze. Finally, as the man handed her the cash, just before she began to turn away, he raised his right hand, brought it to the arm, and scratched vigorously. It was glorious—a victory—and Ilana was hooked on her powers.

By the time she walked out with the babies, three years later, Ilana had turned her bodily troublemaking into a practice, an art. When the girl at the weed spot rolled her eyes at her stankly, Ilana smiled and sent herself to buzz at the girl's inner thigh. And when the Grange Women commented on her hair color or her weight gain at her mother's holiday parties, Ilana chose the falsest of the women, Ann Master, and concentrated on the point of her nose, focusing there until the woman burst into a huge sneezing fit, which eventually turned everyone's stomachs and scattered the party for good.

It was not that Ilana did not like people; she liked most of them well enough. What she didn't like was the way they handled each other. It was all or nothing with most people, a symptom, she felt, of strictly horizontal thought. People either rejected you out of pocket, with an eye-roll and a fake smile, or they insisted on sucking you into a system of fidelities and physiologies—marriages and coituses and births and ceaseless extended-family Thanksgivings—that would bind you to them, wholly, impossibly, forever. Most often they did both, shutting you out and stitching you in at once, which was the cruelest thing of all.

Ilana noticed this pattern first in her family, then in the neighborhood. But as she got older, she saw this schema replicating itself in the halls of her high school, which was nowhere near Harlem and was filled with well-to-do white teenagers who looked nothing like her. So eventually, Ilana took her troublemaking practice to the city streets. She began skipping school to make trips to Alphabet City and the Village, further downtown than most of the Grange teenagers would go, to buy her multi-colored hair at the Wigs & Plus on West 4th, and cans of fuchsia and turquoise spray paint at the Pearl Paint on Canal. Afterward, she would take the 1 & 9 subway line back up to Harlem, where she would tag abandoned buildings with the elaborately drawn names of made-up gangs like "Laydeez Mansion" and "Tha Patriarchy," ducking cops and dealers and anyone else who seemed like they might be part of a real crew. Then would sit on the front stoop of her parents' brownstone, eating cereal, writing rhymes, watching couples and families pass, privately wondering if she would ever make a family of her own.

Mrs. Randolph (whose first name nobody ever said—not even Ilana), did not acknowledge these changes in her daughter. Since George's passing, she had learned to fold her face into a pleasant smile whenever Ilana came up in conversation. She would tell anyone who asked that she and Ilana were doing just fine, thank you, and invite them to her next holiday party.

The dialogues was always more or less the same:

"How's Ilana doin', Mrs. Randolph?" one would ask. "I seen her the other day. Getting *big*, huh? She's got a pretty face, though."

"That girl of yours is *different*, ain't she, Mrs. Randolph?" another would chime in. "But she's smart, though. Quiet ones usually are."

"Well, that's kind of you," Mrs. Randolph would say, standing perfectly still, a stiff smile plastered to her face. "And will we see you at the Arbor Day Almond and Praline Picnic? We'd love to have you there." Then she would walk away, still smiling as primly as she could, whether they'd answered or not.

It wasn't that Mrs. Randolph didn't like people either, exactly. She simply did not like their mess. Never had. As a child, she was often scolded for failing to play well with others, which had always surprised her. In her mind, it was the other children who had turned their noses up at her. If you wanted contact, it seemed to her, the best way to make it was by clear and deliberate request. The improvised rules of hand clapping games and tag tournaments had always been mysterious to her; she never knew when the game was over, or what to do with herself while she waited for her turn to begin. The rise of the make-believe tea party in the first grade was a revelation for her. Unfortunately, by that time, her reputation as an uppity brown-skinned girl had already solidified, and she often found herself sitting in the playground, surrounded by paper napkin place-settings and imaginary teacups, alone.

But later in life, as a professional, a wife, and a mother, her hosting ability had become her most prized trait. By the time she and George had joined the Grange, with its elaborate social protocols and unspoken rules, Mrs. Randolph was certain: the best way to be in touch with the world was by formal invitation only.

The Grange women wondered—well, some of them did—why the woman who could celebrate the wind blowing through her favorite tree and invite the whole of Hamilton Heights to her garden to enjoy it could not part her lips in favor of her own girl.

For this reason and for others, Mrs. Randolph was a neighborhood mystery. She was a thick, sturdy woman with a billowy mass of salt-and-pepper hair, which she kept un-permed and pulled back into a great bush, as enviable as it was strange. She worked as a nurse practitioner at Presbyterian University Hospital, and was also on teaching faculty at the School of Nursing. This always made the Grange Women chuckle, as no one could imagine her breathing warmly over the incapable, much less training young, frenzied nursing students to do the same.

Mrs. Randolph had always been as cool and sharp as a shard of hail, and ever since George died, she'd become even more distant. Everyone remembered the date of George Randolph's passing; it happened on a Saturday, two days before her annual Labor Day Lamb chop Luncheon. Rumor had it the man had keeled over behind the brownstone while Mrs. Randolph pruned the pumpkin leaf centerpieces in the next room. Since then, Mrs. Randolph had floated further and further from the fold, missing most of the Grange meetings and making herself available only by posted RSVP to one of the affairs she held in her small backyard garden.

Mrs. Randolph's affairs always happened outside, regardless of the season. Even in winter, rather than have folks in the house, she rented heat lamps and had the garden's small deck professionally enclosed with temporary tarps so that her guests could sit in perfect warmth amid the gray, dirt-tinged snow. Upon arriving, the women were always ushered quickly through the garden floor parlor, past the kitchen, and into the yard. Some eventually began to take offense at this, and started to speculate as to why no one was allowed to spend time in the Randolph home. It was a major topic of conversation at Mrs. Randolph's last Flag Day Starfish and Striped Bass Fête, the summer before George's death.

"Ain't like it's that pretty a garden," Celia Wallstone had said, craning her head back so that her meaty chin pressed into her neck. "I don't see why we have to have our hoar-durves out there."

"Pssht," replied Sarah Prince, a petite, angular woman. "You know Mrs. Randolph doesn't like too much of people's funk in her furniture. Gets under her skin, you know? And ain't nuthin' generous up under there but a KEEP OUT sign."

"Well I'll tell you," Celia said, stuffing a piece of fish into her mouth. "I'm starting to think KEEP OUT's exactly what we need to do."

In the months after George's death, Mrs. Randolph grew increasingly withdrawn. Ilana grew quieter and stranger, too, until no one saw much of the girl, with the exception of Ann Master, one of the most active Grange members, whose son, DeShawn, had been close with Ilana, against Ann's best efforts. Ann was a slim and well-raised corporate tax lawyer with speckled eggshell skin, which she had always traced vaguely to her "Creole" ancestry, though she wasn't able to provide much more detail on her lineage than that. Luckily, no one ever asked. Ann had always greeted the thought of Ilana with a raised eyebrow. In her view, the girl was born as strange as her mother was mean, and the two seemed to dive miles deeper into their personality flaws when the man of the house passed on. It bothered Ann, as it had bothered all of the Grange women, to see Ilana grow from different to flat-out weird, marching down the streets of Harlem with strangely-colored hair swinging wildly from her head like loose electric wires, mouthing the words to some rap song without a single care as to who was watching.

For most of the fall, Ann tried to be patient with DeShawn regarding his friendship with Ilana. The girl had just lost her father, she reasoned, and consoling her would give DeShawn useful practice in soothing unhappy women, a skill he would need to use as a husband down the line. But around Christmastime, strange things began to happen. Traces of Ilana started to show up in places where the girl herself could not have been. It started with a few strands of synthetic blue extension hair coiled in the bottom drawer of Ann's filing cabinet at work. Then a handful of green press-on nails appeared in her grocery bag, lodged between the pine nuts and the Stahmann's candied pecans. When a whole turquoise braid turned up on the seat beside her on the subway, its end wrapped around the nozzle of a spray paint can, Ann forbade DeShawn from saying so much as "yo" to the girl. She put her foot down, telling him that he was risking his allowance, his college fund, and his future, for what that was worth. And as far as she was concerned, that had been that.

With the exception of Ann, most of the Grange Women had little-to-no contact with Ilana and her mother in the months before the babies. Still, it didn't take more than two eyes and a scrap of sense to know that something was amiss with those two. That was not the sort of thing you would speak on, of course, at least not to a woman's face. So, after Mrs. Randolph missed her fourth consecutive Grange meeting, with the excuse that she was planning her annual MLK Day Mountaintop Mutton Supper, the Grange Women resolved to discuss the matter over Copeland's Sunday Brunch.

"Poor girl," Mary Pitts said, pointing her lips and sloshing the butter around in her grits. "No wonder she acts so strange. Mother can't speak a good word on her to save her life."

"Since the father passed, seem like the girl don't have nobody." Celia Wallstone shook her head, raking the stiff ends of her wig over her shoulders. "Course George didn't hardly say nothing when he was around. Guess that woman scared him so. Nice man, though." She took a sip of her coffee, her eyebrows raised behind the steam.

"Well, I imagine most of what goes on in that house ain't 'zactly what you'd call normal," said Wilma Fridelle, folding her napkin and placing it on the table. "You know they talk on the phone."

"What's that have to do with anything, Wilma?" Said Joyce Turner, a round brown-skinned woman with dread locks and a face as slick as a gumball.

"I *mean*," Wilma retorted, "they call each other on the phone. From one room to the other." She surveyed her audience and sighed. "Rather than go see each other in person. I saw it when I was there for the last Juneteenth Champagne Toast and Jubilee. Come to think of it, I don't think I ever seen all three of them in the same room for more than fifteen minutes, even when George was alive."

"Mmm. It's a shame," Sarah Prince said, leaning into the table. "You know, it means something that he died of bone cancer. Lungs just as airy as springtime, prostate and pancreas you could bet money on, and he ups and dies of poisoned bones. Who ever heard of that? Seems to me living in that house ate him up from the outside in is what happened." She shook her head and dropped her hands in her lap for emphasis.

Ann Master was silent during these sessions, for fear she might be charged with hypocrisy. DeShawn often made news on the whisper mill for small things like graffiti-ing church stairs or stringing his FILA sneakers up on telephone poles for no reason she could think of. But DeShawn was ultimately harmless, and much better than most of these upper-Harlem kids. He had been a member of the Boy's Choir of Harlem, and sometimes she still heard him singing, almost as sweetly, in his bedroom at night. He still liked school well enough, and did almost of all his homework, as far as she could tell. For a teenage boy, he hadn't given Ann much trouble, and, now, watching him grow tall and lean as a walking stick, Ann had started to wish she'd had more children. Frequently, she dreamed of the bland, mealy smell of baby formula and the feel of hot milk splashed for temperature testing against her wrist.

But now, at forty-four, these pleasures of motherhood were lost to her. In recent years, her hips had begun to spread lazily out and down toward her knees, and her small breasts had grown resigned, and had slid down her torso like two little globs of paint on a wall. It seemed the generation to whom motherhood remained—the Talk Show Girls, as she thought of them, with their fake hair and their cheap, gold-plated nose-rings—was completely unequipped to handle the job of procreation. Lately, Ann caught herself sighing audibly at the turned backs of these young mothers as they lifted to their tip-toes to reach high shelves in the grocery store. On bad days, she caught herself looking over her shoulders, eying hungrily their unmanned strollers and basinets.

She had even begun to curse her flighty sister, Lenae, now thirty, for having had five children and made no real efforts to support them. Lenae spent her time pursuing worthless scraps of men and mindless, menial jobs with which she only barely managed to make a living. Had Ann been blessed to have young children at this stage in her life, she often thought, she would make motherhood her art. But now, even though her spirit was willing, her body was not; and moreover, there were no men in sight. DeShawn's father was a useless man who thought sending a pack of subway tokens on Christmas constituted child support, and no other men showed interest. All she could do, Ann decided, was mother the child she had, keep him away from crack, the police, and bad women, and pray he would one day find a decent girl give him the family he longed for.

"That house is strange for sure," Ann said finally, dabbing her napkin at the corners of her mouth. "It's no wonder that girl turned out the way she did."

"What you mean, Ann?" Joyce asked haughtily. She sucked in her round stomach and smoothed her blouse down as if to keep her gut from view.

"Well, now, I'm not *saying*," Ann began. "I'm just saying, you know, Ilana Randolph is not quite like these other young people."

"You mean she's not simple?" Marietta Mann ventured, pushing a cube of melon onto her fork.

"No," Said Celia Wallstone. "She means the girl don't talk, right Ann?"

"Well," Ann said, brushing crumbs from her lap. "I don't like to tell tales, but you know she isn't a woman yet."

"How's that?" Wilma Fridelle and Sarah Prince asked in unison.

"I mean," Ann said, her face going hard with impatience. "She's going on seventeen and hasn't had her—her *visitor* yet. She told DeShawn she didn't plan to either. Said it just like that: 'I don't plan to.'"

"Hmph." Joyce snorted. "If that's true, that's the kinda thing make you think twice before sitting at someone's table. I don't care how good the greens are."

Mary Pitts sucked her teeth and chuckled. "Naw, can't be. Keep talkin,' Ann."

Ann shrugged. "I'm just telling you, is all," she said, folding her napkin and placing it on the table. "Believe it or don't."

It didn't matter that Ilana never heard these conversations herself—she only needed to read the women's stiff smiles when they greeted her. She would think about what the Grange Women must say about her and her mother as she lay in bed at night, gazing up at the dolls that encircled her bedroom, their plastic faces caked with dust.

In her almost-seventeen years of life, Ilana had amassed an impressive crew of teddy bears, My Little Ponies, black Barbie dolls, and others. There were handmade rag dolls with black yarn hair and skin that had thinned to the texture of old paper bags. There were antique brown china dolls with painted swirls of black hair and eyes that closed lazily when jostled, as though silly with delight or begging for sleep. Her favorite had been a brown-skinned, bushy-haired doll with a gleaming white faux-fur jacket that engulfed it like a marshmallow, and with perfectly round bubble-gum colored dots on its cheeks.

Until Ilana was four or so, the dolls had been her peers. She had once enjoyed waking up on Saturday mornings, spreading her blanket on the floor and joining her dolls for mornings of cold cereal and cartoons. But when her classmates began to refer to their dolls as their sons and daughters, Ilana was done. She stopped combing their hair, stopped offering them cereal, stopped taking them to swim in the bathroom sink. She let their eye sockets cake with dirt, let dust settle deep into their fur and hair. She had never bothered to box them, perhaps out of laziness. She simply let them lounge atop her desk and dresser, sit in her chairs, hang from her mantle, and press their paws and fingers against her window sills as they pleased.

Still, for years, the dolls kept coming as gifts from her mother, and from cousins and uncles too distant to know that, ever since age four, Ilana had had no interest in dependents.

Now, under the watch of the dolls, she would think of the Grange Women. She would think about what tragedy of life must have made them who they were—what error kept Joyce Turner's lips running and eyes darting in her doughy face as though calamity would come if she let her mind be still? What indiscretion made Marietta Mann so quiet she seemed to be shocked by the sound of her own breath? These women had been defeated, it seemed, by the quest to fall in line with domesticity's parade—find a good man, find a good job, keep both, have good children that would be willing to lather, rinse, repeat. But the cost of this process, the lint in the trap, seemed always to be the women themselves. Their imaginations, their joys, the brightness of their smiles all seemed to vanish in the tumble of family life, and so they found themselves empty, their bodies warn to laundry bags for other peoples' futures.

So Ilana decided to do things differently. She would handle life selfishly, and never give it to anyone. Sometimes, she was sure of it: she would create no family, no children, nothing but herself. She would consider sharing that selfish life with somebody else only if she truly and deeply felt like it. In the meantime, she would make the ornate ballet of Harlem's social life her entertainment. She would live life, make trouble, and enjoy herself.

The most delicious of her plans involved DeShawn Master, whose mother was arguably the primmest and most anxious of the Grange Women, and who himself was smart and, truth be told, pretty cute. Ilana had seen him for the first time in a while at her father's funeral, six months before the babies, and had immediately come down with a terminal crush, though not the typical kind, she was sure. Most of the Hamilton Heights girls admired DeShawn for the regular reasons: he was known for his deep red skin only lightly peppered with pimples, his pretty voice and his elaborate tags on the walls of the abandoned school on 145th Street. But he was also rumored to have single-handedly masterminded the Destino 2000, a phantom gang whose only real criminal activity was spray painting neon-colored peonies over parking signs and turning traffic signals the wrong way. This, more than anything, made Ilana swoon.

She plotted her first major encounter with DeShawn carefully. It was no small feat; DeShawn was a senior at the rough-and-tumble Catholic boys' school in the Bronx, and Ilana was tenth-grader at her small, artsy nerd-nest on the Upper East Side. There was no chance of unplanned encounters outside of Harlem, and given Mrs. Randolph's awkward standing in the Grange, to trade on their neighborly connection wouldn't have been much help either.

After weeks of planning, Ilana decided to meet DeShawn on his own terms. She skipped school for a week and left the house each day with spray cans, stencils, box cutters, and colored chalk stuffed in the bag where her textbooks should have been. Starting at the rock wall on Riverside Drive where DeShawn and his friends smoked weed after school, she began to place ornate, sprawling letters in paint so thickly glossed it shimmered under the streetlamps. She painted these letters beside the Destino 2000 tags, working her way south and east from the Hudson, past her home off of Amsterdam Avenue, past the Grange office, moving north with DeShawn's flowers as her guides until she reached the row of tidy brownstones on 145th and Convent, where Ann Master's home sat proudly on the corner. There, she swapped the spray cans for the chalk, crouched to the pavement, and placed the biggest and most elaborate letter yet—a lemon-yellow *I,* winking with glints of peach and lime.

It took only two days for news of Ilana's work to wash back on the whisper mill. ShaLondra Prior, a slim tenement girl from Broadway known for her involved and frequently-changing hairstyles, suspected Ilana immediately. ShaLondra had been DeShawn's girlfriend in the sixth grade, and had maintained a de-facto claim over him since then, at least in her own view. She approached Ilana one afternoon, her hair pulled into thick, mile-long box braids and piled on top of her head like Janet Jackson's in *Poetic Justice.* Ilana looked up as ShaLondra neared the stoop, then turned back to her cereal.

"Do you know the bitch who's fucking with Destino?" ShaLondra demanded, patting at her temples.

Ilana shook her head and studied her Craklin' Oat Bran.

"That's some weird shit, yo," ShaLondra said. "It's just a bunch of random letters. What the fuck is an *L* or an *E* supposed to mean anyway?" She watched Ilana's face for a beat. When Ilana said nothing, ShaLondra pursed her lips, pivoted on her heel and turned away, the burnt ends of her braids taking flight behind her.

Ilana knew then that she was on the right track.

The next morning, she marched to Ann Master's house, armed with her paints and stencils. She posted herself behind a dumpster on the corner and waited for Ann to leave for work. When Ann was out of view, Ilana pulled her tools from the bag and shook a can of silver paint as vigorously as she could, its metal agitator ball rattling loud just beneath DeShawn's bedroom window on the first floor. The window rose as though on command.

"What the fuck, Ilana?" DeShawn mumbled, his voice still gravelly with sleep. "I knew that shit was you. All them *I*s and *F*s and shit. What the fuck is that supposed to mean? And, anyway, how you gonna tag my mother's house, though?"

"Oh, you live here?" Ilana said, still shaking the can. "I didn't know. Plus, rhododendrons and azaleas don't exactly say 'step off.' I halfway thought Destino 2000 was a group of kindergarten girls." She shook the can again.

"But damn, why you gotta be so loud?" He mumbled through a smile. "Hold on." And he came downstairs in flip flops, socks, and basketball shorts to let her in.

He rolled a blunt, and the two spent the day writing rhymes and blowing smoke out of Ann Master's parlor window, taking care not to disturb the masks and statues that decorated the room, or to ash on the Strohmenger & Sons piano, which was polished to an indignant shine. When enough time had passed and DeShawn seemed high enough to have forgotten himself, Ilana turned to him and traced her fingernails between the hairs on his knee. She tilted her head to the side, pushed her chin toward him, and softened her lips for a kiss, but DeShawn jerked away.

"No," he said, his voice unsteady. "I mean, that can't happen. You're cool but, you know. My mother and shit… She wouldn't… you're not…"

He continued to stammer, beginning explanations and stopping mid-sentence, gathering his voice and trying again, but Ilana didn't need to hear the words. The next day, she called DeShawn to tell him that it was okay, that she understood what he'd meant, and that she still wanted to be friends.

In the following months, she established a tight liaison with DeShawn. The two skipped school together, tagging buildings and writing songs, stealing icies from the coco helado man while it was still warm and snatching knishes from the hot dog trucks in Central Park when it got cooler. By January, Ilana had succeeded in becoming his truest homie. They even had their kiss, and a few others here and there, but Ilana assured him each time that she wouldn't mention that to anyone. Even when ShaLondra Prior gusted up to her stoop one day, a fresh weave of auburn curls floating behind her like rings in a ringtoss, and said "yo, what the fuck is up with you and D?" Ilana only stirred her cereal and said "What do you mean? We're just peoples," and watched ShaLondra spangle away. Ilana understood what their touching meant, she told DeShawn: nothing.

In those months, she made herself a fixture in Ann Master's home. Ann would return from work many evenings to find Ilana and DeShawn sitting on her front steps, scrawling in their notebooks and moving their heads back and forth in synch like a pair of twin gulls. Ilana enjoyed watching Ann struggle to be pleasant with her. It was a sweet irony, Ilana felt. The imperious restraint that made Ann hate Ilana also kept her from voicing her disdain. No matter what Ilana did, Ann would greet her with the same arched eyebrows, the same squinting eyes, the same dismal lip-raise that strained to pass for a smile. It was a good exercise for the woman, Ilana decided. She began to imagine herself as Ann Master's personal trainer, forcing her into a calisthenics of the spirit. She pulled strands of synthetic hair from her rainbow-colored packs and stuffed them in the crevices of Ann's bags, tied them around the clasps of her necklaces, stuck them down into the legs of her daysheer pantyhose. She watched Ann's smile grow stiffer and her face more flustered each time she saw her—progress, in Ilana's book. Sometimes, DeShawn would report finding whole braids in the cupboards, where Ilana hadn't planted anything at all. Ilana didn't quite understand it, but she didn't complain.

It was gratifying to watch her efforts work on Ann, but Ilana hadn't anticipated annoying DeShawn as well. He confronted her one afternoon as they smoked blunts sitting on the fence at Edgecombe park. "For real, I wish you'd stop fucking with her. I know it's nothing, but still. She's an unhappy woman," he explained, blowing smoke over the park's stony cliff. "She's lonely. You don't like people, so you wouldn't understand about loneliness."

Ilana stopped going to school shortly after that

conversation. It wasn't a decision so much as it was something she observed, as though on the TV screen. She saw herself waking up day after day, the silly morning DJs on the hip-hop station bantering in her ear for only a few minutes before she turned the radio off, rolled over, and continued to sleep. With the exception of a few forays to the Crown Fried Chicken around the corner, she recused herself from the world and retreated to her room.

During those weeks, Ilana spent time with her dolls, and nearly no one else. DeShawn became distant, too, and soon new rumors foamed up on the whisper mill—some saying that he was dating a light-skinned girl from Stuyvesant High School, others saying that ShaLondra Prior was pregnant with his child.

Mrs. Randolph did not notice her daughter's transition into sloth, so busy was she conducting the quiet symphony of her own life, which had become a different thing to manage now that George was gone. Like always, she rose promptly at five every morning in order to press her clothes, smooth her billowy hair into a bun, and take the subway to work at 6:30, not returning until after nine. Sometimes she looked at Ilana and wanted to ask her something, to touch her shoulder or perhaps to give her a hug. But it had always been difficult to talk to Ilana about her day, because the girl was so quiet and because, well, how did one talk to a teenager about anything, really, anyway? And now, it seemed that George's absence had become a film between them, making it impossible for each to see the other clearly, or even to talk to each other, much less to touch.

Then, one Saturday afternoon, while mopping the floors outside of Ilana's bedroom, she decided to peek in. If she could not get to her daughter, she reasoned, just going into her room might be a start. Ilana had left the house hurriedly to go who-knew-where, and though she had no idea when she would be back, Mrs. Randolph took her time surveying the room. But, taking stock, she was horrified. Her good mahogany dresser and vanity were covered in pen marks and paint stains, and smears of electric blue and green chalk clung shamelessly to her elegant salmon-colored walls. Pens and spray cans rolled lackadaisically over her antique rug, surely an injury waiting to happen to anyone who ventured up to the room in the first place.

It had been a beautiful room once, but there was so little to be admired here now. This was the thing with teenagers, she thought. Their vision was so clouded with the dramas of their own lives that they failed to see the very real dangers before them—for Ilana, not just death-by-spray-can, but also the long and lonely life of a woman unconcerned with keeping house. But Ilana had not always been that way—Mrs. Randolph was almost sure of that. Ilana had never been as neat as Mrs. Randolph would've liked, but as a girl she'd always used her creativity around the house to good result, decorating her bedroom room with symmetrical—if tacky—drawings of rainbows and flowers, and bringing beautifully-iced cupcakes to school whenever there was a birthday. And then there were the doll babies, which Ilana had treated with a meticulous love as a child. She had talked to them, bathed them, fixed their hair and clothes with a fastidious and thorough interest that even Mrs.

Randolph had struggled to understand. And even though she'd neglected them later, she never threw them away.

Mrs. Randolph looked for the dolls, ready to admire the collection she'd amassed for Ilana, to feel the hope of those decades of floral print dresses, the years and seasons of perfect pinafores, the generations of patchwork in the oldest dolls' blouses, passed down from her mother to her, to Ilana, maybe still. She wanted to see the touch the yarn hair her favorite doll, to run her fingers over its faux fur jacket, which, only by this lineage of maternal commitment had remained a floury white. It was probably only five minutes or so, but it seemed she'd searched at least an hour before it dawned on her that, in fact, the babies were gone.

The babies were lighter than Ilana had thought they'd be. She made a game of tossing the dolls into the bag, some feet or paws first, some flicked head down like boomerangs or flung like Frisbees, their hair spinning circles of plastic around them. As she worked, she imagined Ann Master waking up to the spectacle she had designed for her: stuffed bears smoking cigarettes on her dining room table, Barbies necking nude on the antique sideboard, ponies in plastic-bag bikinis, soaped up and back floating in her kitchen sink. It would scandalize Ann, shake her from her stupor of meanness, and perhaps even amuse DeShawn a little in the process. They both would suspect her, but it wouldn't matter. She would give Ann Master something more interesting to fret about than the skin tone and temperament of her progeny, and DeShawn would arise, the responsible son, to comfort his mother, joining her in condemnation of strange pranks like this. It was an act of benevolence, really, Ilana decided, and a thoughtful one. She had wrangled his spare key weeks ago in preparation, so there would be no broken windows, and no real need to call the cops. Ann might call Mrs. Randolph, but that didn't worry Ilana; she had grown used to her mother's expressions of bewildered disappointment by now. Tomorrow, after the dust settled and the spectacle had sunk in, DeShawn would throw the dolls away, have the locks changed and renew their lapsed security system account. Then he would call Ilana out of obligation to his mother, under the guise of threatening her, but really, the two would probably share a chuckle. Perhaps that chuckle would even lead to more.

At two a.m. that morning, the streets were quiet and everyone outside was moving. As she walked down the block, she saw that this was because the cops were out, sprinkled in pairs under the awnings where the dealers and other corner-dwellers usually stood. The cops' presence cast an even quiet over the pavement, making the neighborhood seem still and almost false, like a replica of a Harlem that had never really existed. This kind of quiet usually meant that something was going on in the neighborhood's busy world of crack addiction, migration, and desperate economic exchange. The night was sharp with a sense of something underground emerging, something hidden, happening or about to happen. She tightened her grip around the bag and pushed forward down the block.

She had just made out the spokes of the Masters'

front gate when she heard a series of loud pops behind her, like a run of burst balloons. The noise was gone just as quickly as it came, and soon there was more stillness. Ilana thought it was a scare—a child maybe, playing with firecrackers on his mother's stoop. But as her foot hit the pavement in front of DeShawn's house, the popping struck up again, now so close that she thought she could feel the sound brushing the back of her neck. She turned around to see the feet of several men and a couple of women flailing, running in all directions just paces behind her. The silence of the evening broke into a garble of noise: a man grunted loudly and heaved, a woman shouted *"Get the fuck..."* then stopped short, choking on air.

Ilana ran like she hadn't run in years. She felt her fingers flex and air smack cool against her empty palms as the bag fell. Tripping over yarn curls and dingy cheeks, she ran, leaving brown plastic fingers grasping upward in vain. She stepped on the gleaming white fur jacket of her favorite doll and kept going. She felt free in the running, like a small part of something large, a streak of sound in a furor. Hands open, she ran away in a jumble of runners, wondering, as they all did, what had happened—what would happen—and then wondering privately, to herself, if a life could feel this way.

Two weeks later, Ilana still had not heard from DeShawn. She wondered if Ann had seen the torn bag and scattered parts in front of her stoop, but there was no way to find out. The whisper mill was totally silent on the issue. She had heard a little about the gunshots that night—that they had to do with a bad crack deal a few days earlier and a dirty cop who had unexpectedly gone straight. But Ilana heard nothing about the babies. There were no tales of plastic limbs trampled by police boots, no reports of fake baby bottles or miniature pacifiers strewn about Sugar Hill. She walked down to Convent Avenue several times, looking for scraps of yarn hair or scrambling plastic eyes, the white fur jacket growing black in the gutter. But there was nothing—nothing beyond the multi-colored crack vials, newspaper pages, and quarter juice containers that normally ornamented the streets.

Ann Master, too, was absent after the babies. Ilana hadn't expected to see her right away, but she thought, for sure, that she would be at her mother's next party, at least. But Mrs. Randolph's Abolition Day Ice Cream Affair came and went, and no one in attendance had seen skin nor scowl of Ann.

The crowd was much thinner than her mother had expected, which meant less for Ilana to do. It was April, but still cool, and so Mrs. Randolph had ordered heat lamps as usual. Ilana spent most of that afternoon standing at the garden doorway, just close enough to feel the rented warmth on her nose and knuckles. She listened for some mention of Ann Master or DeShawn, but none came. The women talked incessantly about their children and their jobs, what they had planted in their window boxes, what new curtains they would hang for the spring. The ones who had husbands bragged and complained about them; the ones who didn't pushed cranberries through their baked brie, gazing out at the heaps of melting snow.

Occasionally, she caught her mother's eye as Mrs. Randolph flitted around the walled garden, arranging seat cushions and plucking unused name cards from the tables, assessing her spare spate of guests. In those moments, she tried to offer her mother a look of reassurance, solidarity. But each time, Mrs. Randolph looked away.

May 1st was George Randolph's birthday, and though she would not say it, Mrs. Randolph had been dreading the day since she closed the door behind the last guest at the Abolition Day affair. Conveniently enough, May 1st was also May Day in the continental states, and Lei Day in Hawaii. She'd never been to Hawaii and didn't particularly care for false flowers or canned pineapple, but those things did remind her of George—queer, comical George who insisted on wearing floral print socks tucked into his Oxfords because, as he put it, one always had to have "a little whoo-ha" on one's person to make the day worthwhile. George was capricious and unpredictable, but he always carried his strangenesses out silently, like Ilana. Mrs. Randolph appreciated this quality of his more than she had been able to articulate when he was alive. His silence allowed her to enjoy the weirdness of him, in a way, the strange thing of him made wonderful, because it was reserved only for her.

And so, in this spirit—George's, and Ilana's—she decided to host her first May Day/Lei Day Luau. She could not be seen dragging a dead pig through the streets of Harlem, so she determined that a beef brisket would have to do. The pineapples would be fresh and the flowers would be real, and there would be May Day baskets full of prettily-iced cakes and cookies for the sweet-eating Grange Women, under the pretense, of course, that they were for any children who happened to come by. The turn-out at the April affair hadn't been the best, but people were surely sick with the long winter and the slow change of seasons. And regardless, she thought, who wouldn't come out for cookies, Hawaiian lays, and slow-braised beef? There was something for everyone in that—*Fun for the Holy Families!* is what George would say. A May Day/Lei Day Brisket and Basket Luau. She let the idea caramelize in her mind.

On the morning of the Luau, the sky over Hamilton Heights was as clear and blank as an ice cube. No one had RSVP-ed for the event yet, though Mrs. Randolph asked for the appropriate one-week's response on the invitations. She attributed this lapse in etiquette to an unfortunate triumph of Colored People's Time—a condition that sometimes reared its scruffy head even in the best circles—and so she went on about the preparations. She cleaned and covered the tables, pinned the seat cushions in place, and directed the installation of the makeshift luau pit, watching as delivery men spread bags of dirt over her yard's limestone floors. She put out the baskets, filled them with reasonably expensive pastries, and strung fresh carnations into necklaces no one had signed up to wear.

Ilana watched quietly and from a distance, saying nothing as Mrs. Randolph prepared for the event, her spine curved into a question mark over the stove, muttering her dissatisfaction at batch after batch of Hawaiian pasta salad. It didn't matter that the production was a waste of time. The work kept her

mother busy and distracted—perhaps happy, even—
and it seemed pointless and cruel to take that from her.
Still, it had stung to see how poorly attended the April
event was, and it was even harder to see her mother at
it again. So Ilana stuffed a few spray bottles into her
backpack and left the house, offering to bring back a
bag of ice when she came home.

When she returned that afternoon, the house was
tinkling with sound. The laughter of several voices
lunged forward, not from way out in the garden, but
from right there, chiming thickly through the first
floor. When Ilana pushed through the French foyer
doors, she saw Mrs. Randolph sitting in the middle of
the dining room, stiff as a scarecrow, a field of little
bodies waving around her.

There were children. Children and more children
of various ages: prim toddlers in cornrows and
overalls, a messy nine-year-old with distressed Afro-
puffs and a floral-print skirt. Some clutched juice
boxes or stuffed animals, others held hands, their tight,
well-greased box braids brushing the hem of Mrs.
Randolph's ivory tablecloth. One child, a girl, wore a
crisp white faux-fur jacket that looked freshly
scrubbed to gleaming, save for what seemed to be a
faded foot print on the left arm.

When she stepped into the dining room, Ilana saw
that Ann Master was there too, holding a leaky-nosed
infant on the table before her, the bulge of its diaper
resting squarely on Mrs. Randolph's white lace runner.
And there beside her was DeShawn, careening on the
two side legs of Mrs. Randolph's mahogany chair to
help a child with bright pink cheeks tie her shoe.

"Mrs. Master and her family decided to stop by

and surprise us," Mrs. Randolph said to Ilana, her face trick-knotted into a smile. "Isn't that nice?"

Ilana nodded and looked at DeShawn, who tied the shoe and hoisted the child onto his knee. The sideboards were covered with folded cloth napkins and baskets of cookies, and a large pitcher of bright purple juice sat uncovered at the edge of the table. Ilana eyed the juice pitcher, so wide and brazen against the thin white cloth.

"It's so nice to see you, Ilana," Ann said, wiping the infant's mouth with its bib. The baby gave a wet gurgle. "It's been such a long time. We've really missed having you around." The was a casual sweetness in Ann's tone that made Ilana think Ann might have forgotten herself—that she might actually believe she liked Ilana after all.

Ilana nodded and tried to offer some kind of smile. She looked at DeShawn over the mass of children—five, altogether, she now saw, though they felt to her like many more. DeShawn began to bounce the fur-coated child on his lap. The girl gave a flurry of giggles, her black eyes rolling with delight.

"So you were saying, Ann? About your sister?" Mrs. Randolph placed another basket of cookies on the table and walked to the sideboard, trying, Ilana could tell, not to seem too eager for details.

"Well, yes, like I said. They just showed up on the stoop one morning, a few weeks ago now," Ann said, her face firm and bright as a pat of butter. "All of them together, and Lenae nowhere in sight. I do wish she'd sent word in advance, but you know—some people just don't know how to be." She shifted the child onto her knee and sighed. "Of course, I was worried at first, with all the things that go on around here. There was a shooting just the night before they got here, right there on my block." She switched the child to the other knee and patted its behind. "But children need mothers, and women need children, is what I told DeShawn. Men need them, too, whether they know it or not."

Ann looked at DeShawn, who nodded dutifully, smiling awkwardly as though he were posing for a photo. Sitting side by side amid a sea of children, their slim faces cast in twin smiles, DeShawn and Ann looked like two halves of a quotation mark. Ilana had never seen DeShawn look like this before. Her disappointment surprised her.

"Well, we had to fix them up, of course," Ann continued. "They were a bit discombobulated, at first." A child waddled by and Ann stopped it with her free hand. She licked her finger, cleared a smear of cookie frosting from one of the pink cheeks, and released it to its game. "But we're having a good time putting them together, aren't we?" She wiggled the infant's booted toe, and the baby reached up and put its palm on her face. DeShawn bounced the child in the fur coat again and gave his picture-day smile.

"Reminds you of how it was when *they* were young, doesn't it, Mrs. Randolph," Ann said, gesturing with her eyebrows to DeShawn and Ilana, the child's fingers still on her nose.

"Well, yes," Mrs. Randolph said.

Suddenly, the child in the fur coat leaned forward in DeShawn's lap, slunk down to a standing position, and lunged for a basket of cookies, tripping over a buckle in the rug and sending the basket, the napkins, and the plastic juice pitcher crashing to the floor. Everyone watched as purple juice spread slowly over the rug and began to sink in. The child grabbed onto Mrs. Randolph's skirt and hoisted herself up again, leaving a wide smear of purple liquid and cookie grease on the pale gray cotton.

Ilana hurried to the foyer closet for cleaning supplies, and DeShawn moved beside her mute, almost automated. She handed him a rag and a bottle of cleaner. As the two ducked down to the floor, she checked his face, hoping to share an eye roll or a smirk at the ridiculousness of the situation, but he did not look up, except briefly, to offer a wild, panicked smile she couldn't decipher.

When the spot was cleaned, Mrs. Randolph began moving the remaining baskets and tablecloths to the sideboard. Ilana waited for the moment when Mrs. Randolph would put the visit to an end, ushering the newly-sprawling mess of the Masters out of her house. She couldn't imagine her mother taking much more of this disorder, and for the first time, Ilana was glad.

"Oh, Mrs. Randolph, I'm so sorry about that," Ann said pleadingly. She took the child in her arms and looked sternly into its face. "Tell Mrs. Randolph you're sorry," she said.

"I'm sorry, Miss Mand..." the child stammered, clutching the furry hems of her jacket sleeves. Her face began to tremble, and her eyes grew wet.

"I'm sorry, Miss Man..." she tried again.

Mrs. Randolph scrubbed at her skirt, hunched over at the sideboard, and Ilana imagined the look of trussed-up horror that would show on her face when she turned back around. But when she finally turned toward the group again, her expression was smooth and easy. Ilana even thought she saw a smile beginning to sprout between her mother's cheeks.

"That's alright, sweetheart," Mrs. Randolph said quietly. "Here." She held a bright pink cookie in the air. "Now, remember: next time, just say 'May I have a cookie?'"

"May I have a cookie, Miss Man-off?" The child repeated. Mrs. Randolph nodded. She placed the cookie at the center of a napkin, and gave it over. "Yes, you may. And my name is Joy."

Ann Master beamed, her smile so thick it could have oozed from a tube. DeShawn took this as his chance to jump in, prodding the child: "Say, 'Thank you, Mrs. Joy,'" which the child did between mouthfuls.

"Very good," Mrs. Randolph said in a lilt. "That's right. You're welcome." Ann smiled.

A brightness shone in Ann's and her mother's eyes as they instructed the child gleefully in the social choreography of this house, this neighborhood, this world—*Say, 'Please, Mrs.' Say 'Thank you, Mrs.' Oh yes. Very good. That's right*—while the child tugged, uncomfortable or oblivious, at the wisps of fur on its jacket. Once, in the sixth grade, Ilana had read a novella about a quirky but likeable girl who complained of always being an outsider in her neighborhood. Throughout the first hundred pages of the book, the girl joked self-deprecatingly about feeling like an alien, only to find out in the final third that she actually *was* an alien, completely unrelated to anyone she'd ever known, come on special assignment from another planet to observe social life on earth and write a report about it. Watching her mother and Ann transform bizarrely in front of her, Ilana felt how that girl must have felt: nauseated and relieved at once.

DeShawn bent to gather the wet rags and Ilana moved with him, eager to be out of sight.

"Look at them," Ann said to Mrs. Randolph, her voice heavy with conspiratorial warmth. "Won't be long before they're having babies of their own." She darted her eyes first at DeShawn and then at Ilana.

Mrs. Randolph nodded, her smile full-on now.

"Ilana—" Ann and Mrs. Randolph said in unison. Then they laughed. Mrs. Randolph's laugh was timid at first. But Ann's was deep and hearty and from the gut, and Ilana could hear her mother's laugh start to take root, too.

"Why don't you join us?" Ann said, moving the baby bag aside and patting the cushion of the seat next to her.

"Yes." Mrs. Randolph looked up at Ilana, her face simpler and stranger than it had ever looked before. "You should. Feel free."

Ilana paused, wishing she could take a picture of the moment and keep it in her pocket for later—a havoc of babies wreaked on her mother's dining room floor, two Grange Women merrily peeling layers off themselves to put things back in order, and all this the work of several utterly uninvited guests. She felt happy enough for the people that filled the room, but thrilled for her own freedom to leave it. She regretted only that there was no one she could tell the whole story to.

"No, thank you," she said, her voice a polite perfection.

A child whined and a baby gurgled as Ilana walked around the brownstone, gathering her box cutters and her spray cans, placing them carefully in her backpack, one by one. By the time she made it back down to the vestibule, the laughter had struck up again, louder this time, and now DeShawn had joined in. She zipped her jacket, slung her bag over her shoulder, and locked the door behind her, not bothering to say goodbye. The chill of the afternoon sank deep into her skin from all directions, unblocked and unfiltered, against her legs and her empty palms. The chill stayed stayed with her, bone deep, pushing her forward as she walked, and hummed, and reviewed the days.

Ivy

I am a woman
Which means
I am insufficient
I need—
Something to uphold me
Or perhaps uphold.
I am a woman.

— "Ivy," by Georgia Douglass Johnson

I am a woman

Ivy rubbed her stomach, then gathered it up in her hands. It wasn't a stomach so much as a spreading middle, a generous armful of skin and flesh. There were no words for her body. Thick hoof ankles bolstered trunk-like shins that bundled soft brown calves on their backs. Knees, bulging heavy in the front, skied caves of secret young skin behind them. Hips, hands, arms—they were all there, but more and different. Hands thicker than hands. Arms fuller than arms. Hips wider than hips, and busier with weight to carry.

Mostly it was not her body, but everything else that tired her—the world outside, all the things beyond her skin. But then, when she came home and looked at herself with the world's dust still on her eyes, she was often tired still. All that differentness. All that nameless flesh, that wordless body. And on top of everything, her head seemed so small…

Which means

This little white man is looking at me. He is inspecting me on this bus like a woman inspects a pimple on her chest. This white man in his suit is eating his sandwich under the NO FOOD/DRINK/SPITTING/RADIO PLAYING sign on the M4 bus and his eyes are steady on me. He stares, snarls, turns back to his paper, but he can't help but look up again, again, again, peering at me as though he wishes he could reach out, squeeze me, pop me, get me gone. Of course I have seen this man before. There are so many of him. When I was younger—eleven, seven, even five—I swallowed their wishes for me. I remember yearning to press my body until it popped and seeped away, delighting in the dream of my body punctured and gone.

Now I stare back. It's hard, exhausting, but I do. I watch this man, his sandwich in his hand, unallowed and flagrant, his paper on his lap unread, his eyes, unabashed, on me. I imagine a world in which I bow, devour his sandwich, his hand, his body, his briefcase, the bus, and the street, wipe my mouth and bow grandly again. My imagination amuses me. I swallow my laugh into a smile and turn away.

Harlem is big, gorgeous and moving. Strutting its street lights and corner stores, men playing with balls and children carrying groceries for old ladies, church bells ringing the time. Cops, sitting, watch the dealers standing, slinging double-dutch girls into short tight dresses as heads and eyes and genitals follow. "*Excuse me—*" My neighborhood is full. Outside the projects people in t-shirts play cards on cement tables and children chalk the ground in front of swingless swing sets, write their names on monkey bars. "*Excuse me—*" Someone got shot on this corner and there is a mural, a portrait, a cross, candles, flowers, big brown bear with big read heart. My neighborhood is mourning. "*Excuse me—*" I wonder who he was. "*Excuse me—*" Two tall men in pink shorts and braids dance across the street....

"*Excuse me!*"

This older woman whose peers would call her "heavy-set" heaves my thighs with her hips. She is trying to push me into my seat, half a seat too small for me.

I pull in for her, move my feet so she can rest her cane. She surveys me, frowns, then continues to rustle and breathe. The woman makes fists out of her hips and arms and pushes me hard, handles like furniture, banging, shoving. She shifts our weight around in the seats, thrusts into my side, into my thigh. She leans forward, she huffs. I decide to do this dance with her. She is old, black, a woman; she deserves her space. I know that with her violent bending lips and bones she is telling me that I need to try and fit—she has learned this. I press myself into the narrow seat for her and send my mind away.

155

The street numbers are counting seconds half-time and I am almost home. I grasp the metal handrail and hoist myself out of the seat. Glide, aim my weight, pop in a half-guided fall quickly onto the pavement. Hike up jeans, smooth out shirt, I prepare to climb Sugar Hill.

The men on the block are familiar, and their calls mark home like a series of tattered welcome mats.

"Big Girl!" a middle-aged black man in sweatpants calls from beneath the bodega awning.

"*Que linda, la gorda!*" a short Dominican man with sunglasses and a plate of *chicharrones* in his hand calls from a crate in front of a car.

"Excuse me, miss." A young dread clearly smoked into his sixth sense walks up behind me. He follows me quietly until I turn around.

"Can I get your name?" he says. His eyelids are thick as prunes.

I am breathing heavily, out of breath from the climb. I pause, steady myself till I am calm and can smile for him. "Why?" I say, hoping my face is not too sweaty, thanking him silently for calling me "Miss."

"You know, you a pretty girl... Maybe I could take you out sometime, nahmean?"

"My name is Ivy." I smile and feel the thick feather boa of woman glory around my shoulders. He extends his hand.

"Ivy. That's a pretty name." His voice drags. "I'm sayin', Ivy... I like big women. You strong, nahmean? Like you not gon' take no shit. I like that." He gestures strength with a Sumo wrestler pose and slides into place with others like him in my memory. I wish I could paint myself on my shoulders to warn these men that I am fragile, that there are valleys here, and if they are looking for only hills they need not waste their time. Maybe I should get my hair straightened—maybe it would help.

The dread is still talking, making a chorus with the other Harlem men as I walk away. Their eyes feel like borrowed diamonds on my neck and I want to give these men what I have if they want it. But when they smile, I always wonder if they are swallowing laughs.

I am insufficient

On the music video channel, white- and yellow-skinned women jump and fly across the television screen like kernels of popcorn from a skillet, and I watch, waiting for the doorbell to ring. Singing and dancing, the women make declarations about men and love and self, the traps of life. They hold forth on the shedding and catching of various weights as they bounce around the glass box and spring into the air: *losing you was like losing two hundred pounds of nuthin. Love me up like good food, fill me with your love.* I check the clock: only five fifteen. I settle into the sofa's arms and sigh, waiting for my food to come. Waiting for food is a special kind of waiting. A wanting and a not wanting at once.

On all the other channels there are small white people. This one with a small black friend, these two embracing one another, this one gaunt and luxurious and alone. I feel my middle with my left hand and hold the remote with my right. I wish these buttons would take me to some world in which I could find myself in a three-segment struggle complete with mild conflict and total conclusion, love at each stage, a role to play. I am pressing buttons, scanning the screen for myself like a spirit in the air looking for a body on the ground... Nothing. I rest my hand on a warm fold of me and press in.

The black talk-show mother is holding a grown white woman, stroking her mousy brown hair, kissing it, stroking again. The woman's tears and snot are leaving stains on the talk-show mother's suit jacket and the mother invites more. "He's not worth it, baby. You know it. This is about you." The audience claps. The camera pans the spectators and freezes on the most empathic faces: a black man nodding in solemn support, a white girl streaming tears down pink cheeks, an older Latina holding her chest, her eyes moist and proud. The woman sobs: "Thank you. I love you." The talk show mother looks up at the sky and back down at her charge: "I love you, too, baby." The audience claps and claps and claps.

No part of me is clapping, but my eyes moisten. So *this* is the big black woman in the glass box. The closest thing I will ever find to me. She is not bopping and singing and moving like the others. Not discovering life's secrets, falling in or out of love. She instead must *be* love, the vast, wet ground from which generosity grows. I can never be a small, broken white woman; I can never make it my life to love one. I cannot lay down in my own lap and cry; my lap is buried—my middle—so far away.

As I watch, I remember being young, twelve or so, and dreaming of a spotlighted existence as girls do. I thought I could dance around this screen one day, in the same way that I thought all allegories were about me—Alice, Dorothy, Rapunzel, Snow White—their lessons my lessons, their stories all secretly mine. Now I know better—the bus men, the street men, the women behind the screen all see to that. But still there is a small part of me. I feel it now. Stubbornly, hardheadedly, that part of me still waits for the stares and shoving hands to dissolve into light. For mean eyes to soften and crinkle into smiles, for pointing fingers to lift and part and join together in applause.

I watch the talk show mother's eyes shine onto the white girl's cheeks, a spotlight. Nothing but giving in that gaze. I am reminded that *getting* is not supposed to be for me. And then there is the doorbell, the food.

I need—

For Ivy, the man in the doorway had become an awkward acquaintance by now. He knew her number, her address, how to press the broken elevator button hard enough to be carried to her floor. He did not know her name and she did not know his, but there was an intimacy in that too. He knew what she ate and how she liked to eat it. She flashed her smile and hoped he would smile back, hand her the bag, and leave quickly.

"Hello," she said. The tenement hallway smelled like *arroz con guandules*. Someone was cooking down the hall.

"Hi—how are you?" He sat the plastic bag on the doormat and shuffled through his pockets for the receipt. Ivy held out a twenty and waited.

"Fifteen-seventy." He looked up with wide eyes, first at the money, then at her. He lingered on her face for a minute, then took the cash. "Thank you," he said. "You having a good day?"

She shifted her weight and stooped for the bag: warm air, crisp heat.

"Thank you," she said again, the best answer she had.

He nodded, counted the change, and handed it to her, still looking at the bag.

"See you later."

On the television, a reporter stood a few blocks away on the corner of 137th and Frederick Douglass Boulevard, in front of colored lights and a police barricade. She was reporting live from Harlem, she said, where yet another drug-related shooting had taken place. The neighborhood was in panic, she explained, holding her hat to her head as a gust of wind blew her calico hair into her face. She shivered— or was it a stutter? "Harlem r-residents are stricken with fear."

Ivy opened the containers: chicken, broccoli, gravy, egg rolls, rice.

The camera tightened on neighborhood faces.

"Our young people need to learn to stop this mess. We can't keep dying like this."

Ivy spooned rice into her mouth and chewed over the peas and onions: bursts of sweet grease released in gulps.

"I hope the mayor watches this and sees that we need to find ways to keep our kids in school instead of out here on the block."

She steeped the broccoli in its sauce and rested it

on her tongue for a second, chewed and went in for another piece.

"I just can't believe he's gone."

The food warmed her stomach as she watched. There was sadness, there was heartbreak, there was anger, and more. She closed her eyes and listened to Harlem around her: laughter, hip-hop, sirens and bachata. An old soul song. Children calling mothers at windows, men yelling down the street. Ivy did not hear fear, did not see it, except on the face of the reporter herself. But still, here she was, the one with the microphone, her huge eyes at the center of the camera's frame:

"The people of Harlem are in a state of panic."

Ivy finished what was in front of her, heaped the plate with more.

Something to hold me

I would sell my feet for a bed right now. For real. I would resign myself to lay limp for the rest of my life if it would promise me comfort in this one instant. I am dreaming of floating in cool blocks of Jell-O, a pool of thick pudding, even a pile of leaves.

I am at the beauty parlor, in a too-tight chair, being cut into and it hurts. This is not an old, easy pain. I feel those old pains, too, and I can list them at will: bra cutting paper-cut slits into my shoulders, jean waist burning at my middle, ripping my skin raw. Those pains are always happening, are happening now too, but my body stopped feeling them a while ago. This pain is different. This chair...

Last night I ate myself to sleep to the music of

TV and street sounds. People were crying and laughing all around me, and I was quiet inside. Men called my body a hard-sealed woman and I did not speak too loud. I did not scream—I could lay down.

But now I am sitting stuffed into a narrow metal chair, piled, layered, folded like pastry dough into this small space whose stiff arms are denting my sides. The woman behind me is slathering cream on my scalp and it is so cool at first, all snow and mint. But then it starts to burn. And my hips are burning and my behind is numb and I am trying so hard to send my mind away to still and calm last night, to the food warming me from the inside, to my sofa, soft and wide like a lap. But the chair is tearing tracks along my legs and I feel my body gasping.

"It's burning," I say. My voice is as numb as my hips, and I realize I have not spoken in an hour, maybe more. I squeeze myself out of the chair—one side of my body thick and heavy, the other worse. I balance my weight on the counter and stand, looking for the sink. My hips throb with the air, make a rhythm.

"No, baby, wait. You need to keep it in. Let it set for a while."

But my temples are chattering hot, my thighs dead weight beneath me: I can't wait. I lunge in a heavy slow motion toward the shampoo chair. Try to maintain my posture, to not look like a woman in pain. It is an impossible step to manage. I fumble with the knobs, pull the chair away from the plastic sink, try to leave enough room for my back…. I am spilling over the edges, as always….

The woman mutters over me as she rinses the No Lye Relaxer out of my scalp… the water is so good…

"You didn't wait long enough"... my head is crying "thank you" and my eyes are wet... *"Not straight enough, you know, you got too much hair"*... I move from cool and grateful in the water to raw and hot stuffed under the drier... *"Long though—that's good. Long hair slims the face."*

In the row of women under the drier, I am like a mother duck lined with her chicks... small them, small them, small them, Big Me. When the timer ticks and the heat stops I am relieved. I push out of the chair slowly, with one foot, but the chair makes a deep wobble... please... I am sending my soul to wake up my legs and tell them to hold me up before this chair collapses... lord, I do not need this chair to collapse... legs, come on and help... where are you... this chair will not hold me....

"Ok, baby, I'm ready for you, come on now. Let's get at that hair. I can't get it straight as I'd like 'cause you wouldn't let it set, but I can blow it out good and work it with the iron, come on."

I am praying for the strength and grace to get up. I imagine a world in which I do not have to scan every room for something to hold me gently without breaking under my weight... my heart....

Or perhaps uphold.

My scalp is numb and my hair flops against my ears outside. I am trying to feel it as a triumph—of beauty, of womanness, but I can't. My scalp is burnt hard and my hips are aching. I imagine other wants: I want to feel myself in a suit eating a sandwich under a no eating sign, shooting glares like lasers wherever I please. I want to feel myself standing on one of these corners, big-jeaned and beepered, tossing thoughts out my mouth like darts at passers-by. I want to feel myself holding a nice hat in fear. I want to feel myself falling apart in someone's lap, I want to believe they will pull me together, prepare me to live in this world...

I walk uptown past vacant lots and abandoned buildings, men behind tables selling black books and oil, women offering to braid my hair. They see that it is flapping, just straightened, but they offer anyway. I turn at 146th and walk toward the water, kicking broken glass through the streets as I go. At the overgrown park on Edgecombe, I choose the splintered green bench that is missing a slat of wood. The missing slat means I lean can back, spread.

I watch the little league boys play baseball on the other side of the torn metal fence. A tour bus parks behind me and a sea of tourists floods from the door. The boys and I notice them. They boys continue their game. I continue to feel my space and watch. Some of the tourists see me and look away quickly. Their sons point and laugh.... Their fingers are dirty. Their daughters stare.... They are skinny and ugly and to me they look sad.

I try to focus on the game while the tourists press against the fence and take pictures and talk.

"They're so cute, poor things."

The batter hits the ball high, past fat clouds and slim branches. The boy in the outfield catches. Everybody cheers.

"Oh, I can't imagine growing up in such a dangerous neighborhood."

The players drop their gloves and run to each other, exchanging daps and hugs in the patchy grass. I see tourist children laugh at me... in my head I laugh back.

"It really makes you appreciate what you have, knowing that these kids are so unfortunate."

Now everybody runs to the mound, cheering. Some pick up broken tree branches and chase each other around in the dirt. Others grab bottle caps and throw them, laughing.... I smile.... the outfielder sees me and smiles back.... I laugh with the boys.... I can feel my legs. I rub them, feel their thickness.... They feel nice.

I am a woman.

Ivy comes home and pushes her hair back, away from her face. Her eyes are clear half-moons trimmed in fur. She is standing in front of her mirror, filling it to its edges. She lifts her arms, sways in the space around her. She has been standing for a while, feeling the roughness and softness of her body... massaging her middle... scratching her shoulders... reaching inside of her caverns and folds. Her feet are tired, but not too tired. When she wants to move, she will roll and sprawl wildly. And when she is ready, she will lay down.

Adale

The stink of burnt oatmeal seemed to hang from the kitchen's wood beams, perpetually in idle swing like the stray pairs of sneakers that used to hang from the streetlamps outside. Dominique Potter had burnt ten pots of oatmeal among the half-packed boxes in the Harlem brownstone by the second Thursday of 2005. Her mother would have said it was because she was pregnant again—baby brain, she called it—but Dominique knew that wasn't it. Just a few weeks before, she had been known to burn only the outermost oats of a given pot, and those only slightly, so that most of the mush within could be plied with butter or crusted with brown sugar and salvaged after all. Now her five-year-old son, Mandela, had had to wait at the table for an hour each morning while she bent over her belly to turn on the oven, opened its door for heat, poured the first pot of oatmeal, turned to the news, got lost in the tsunami, and let the oats burn. Eventually, she would return to the stove, barely more vigilant but determined to assure the safety of all or most of the second pot of the day. Dominique had spent much of her time in that kitchen since the day after Christmas, packing boxes and cooking meals, preparing for the family's move. She would stand before the stove, her spine curved back and her belly bounding out in front of her, watching homes drift across the television screen like bits of paper on the waves, wondering what kind of place she'd be going to herself, when the family moved with this new baby, in just a few weeks.

Images of ruin lit the television screen those mornings. Pictures of broken bodies, of houses and towns halved and quartered as though bit into by great celestial fangs sat suspended in graphic boxes beside the heads of reporters with perfectly cropped hair and perfectly baffled eyes. During those first few days of the storm, the death toll climbed a little each hour, finally reaching digits she could not quite imagine. *What would one hundred thousand of something look like?* she had thought that Wednesday, just after the storm hit. Silently, she twisted her tongue around the *T*- and *S*-heavy words that splashed from the reporters' mouths like water kicked up from puddles: Sri Lanka. Indonesia. Tsunami. *What would one hundred thousand be?* Stroking her belly, she tried to imagine the one hundred thousand blades of grass the family might find in the Poconos, where they would be moving. She wondered if there could be a hundred thousand stars, crusted in other nights' skies. Her mind crawled and clawed at the numbers on the screen. She planted herself there, among the torn trees and ripped beaches, half-understanding, half-not. Eventually, Mandela would call her back and tell her, sneezing, that their breakfast had begun to burn.

Mandela was very patient those mornings. Each day, he emerged from his bedroom shortly after Dominique woke up. He climbed down the creaking brownstone stairs behind her, and stationed himself at the edge of the long wooden table, his arms stretched across the small corner of wood not yet covered with flat cardboard boxes, his grandmother's trinkets or his grandfather's mail. While Dominique tended to the stove, he sat slumped on his elbows with his short legs stretched beneath the table, watching the television blink and speed in reels off the top of the screen, then return from the bottom, only nanoseconds of action having passed. He did not let his disappointment with the news clips show. They seemed to him to have been exactly the same each morning since Christmas, though they were repeated incessantly for some reason he could not understand, and had even barged in and interrupted his cartoons several times that week. But he said nothing. He was grateful for his cold and his extended Christmas vacation, happy to spend his mornings sneezing here in the air-bitten kitchen, among smell of burnt grains and oven heat, instead of at school.

Mrs. Potter, Dominique's mother, applauded her grandson's patience many times during this vacation. For her, this winter was evidence of a slow crash downward in the life of their family. The loss of her husband's job had combined with the increased cost of living and property tax in the neighborhood, brought in with the new chain stores and the onslaught of developers hungry to hack brownstones into three-family homes. That plus the freeze in her hours at work all came together to break down everything she'd felt was the family's foundation: the heat had to be turned down to a minimum, the house sold, and their Christmas ritual thinned near to nothing.

Most years, since Dominique was a child, Mrs. Potter had seen to it that their tree bulged with gifts, like the white people's family trees in Christmas movies. Every Christmas eve, once the child (Dominique until her 16th birthday, then Mandela the year after) had gone to sleep, Mr. Potter would squat on the living room floor beside the tree, his tools spread around him as he assembled the dream house, the five-part stereo or whatever thing would serve as the center-piece gift that year. Then, returning home from midnight Mass, Mrs. Potter would drag out all of the smaller gifts she had bought over the past year and station herself at the dining room table among rolls of tape and reams of shiny wrapping paper. Most years, it took her hours to wrap all the gifts, cutting little rectangles of paper with which to label each one, signing them "from Mommy and Daddy" at first, then "from Grandma and Pop-Pop." Others were from Santa, marked with notes like "Ho, Ho, Ho, thanks for the cookies!" For the past five years, she had signed the greatest number of gifts from Dominique: "For Mandela, with all my love, Mama."

It became clear early enough on that 2004's Christmas spread would not be so grand. Mr. Potter had lost his management job at the Port Authority earlier that year and was now only days away from seeing his unemployment run out. Dominique's job at the new Pathmark on 145th street paid for her own clothes and groceries for the family, but nothing more. Mrs. Potter's monthly struggle to balance the mortgage, the utilities, and clothing for herself, her husband, and her grandchild on her medical assistant's salary had failed on more than one occasion, so that in

November she had had to establish a new family habit of opening the oven door to save on heat. She had tried to stave off the slimming of their Christmas ritual for years, but this year facts had to be faced: in a contest between housing and Christmas cheer, the mortgage won, hands down.

Mrs. Potter felt the sting of the change most deeply on Christmas morning. Mr. Potter had closed himself off in the living room since the anniversary of his unemployment, leaving her to assemble the meager Christmas spread alone, and so she'd gone to bed in the pre-dawn hours, drained as much from disappointment as from Midnight Mass. Mandela awoke around 5 in the morning, roused by the excitement that seemed to run like bugs over children's skin on that one day each year. She heard him creak from his bedroom, his socked feet scampering down the linoleum-covered stairs to find the spread she was sure would disappoint him: a cheap plastic backpack, three paper-back books about rainforest turtles, and two dubbed and hand-marked C.D.s, all wrapped in last year's paper and arrayed sparsely beneath the tree.

Mrs. Potter awoke that morning prepared to fold the child into her breasts and assure him that things would be better next year, once they had moved out of the city. But when she pushed through the family room door, she found him perched cross-legged on the old brown sofa, a book in his lap, his chin waving merrily to the hip-hop radio station's latest compilation album.

"Grandma," he had said, his mouth gaping wide, displaying his missing front tooth. He tilted his sleep-crusted eyes up at her. "Did you know that snapping turtles can't snatch their heads up under their shells like the other kinds?"

Mrs. Potter shook her head and invited the boy to come with her to the kitchen where she could start dinner while he told her all about it. She hoped that this next grandchild would be so patient. Rent at the Sterling Pocono Glenn was cheap—less than half their mortgage now—but still she was not entirely sure that even two or three years of low-cost and tax-free living would repair the family's situation. She hoped her granddaughter would somehow take more after her brother than Dominique, that she would share Mandela's maturity, his measured perspective and his balanced sensibility not unlike Mrs. Potter's own. It had been Mandela, after all, who silenced his disconsolate twenty-one year-old mother when Mrs. Potter informed the family that they would be losing the house.

"Now that things are finally getting nice around here, of course we have to leave," the girl had shrieked, bouncing to her feet and pushing the dining room table away from her as though it had provoked her to fight. "As soon as some good stores show up and the place starts looking better. Now that people are starting to give a shit about us, now we have to go." She had turned to Mrs. Potter then, her eyes sharp as box cutter blades. "And what about Adale? You want her to grow up out in the sticks in an apartment building so cheap it advertises on TV? No black people around, no stores, no music. Not even any real streets! Or did you forget about her?"

Mrs. Potter did not respond to her daughter's tantrum, except by dabbing the meat sauce off of

Mandela's cheeks and standing up to clear the table. Mr. Potter, too, stayed silent, filling his glass with water and raising it to his face to crunch on ice. Only Mandela had spoken. He pushed himself to the edge of his chair at the foot of the table, lifted his head, and said quietly:

"Maybe she'll like the country, Mama."

Dominique let her friends believe she had named Mandela for his father, a corner crack slinger named Nelson. It was a convenient explanation—her friends thought it was a smart way to make the boy a junior without giving him such a corny name. They liked the way Mandela sounded, too, although Rashida and Yunnique said it might be too effeminate and worried that he might have to make up for it in wildness or extreme intelligence to avoid being beaten up. But really, Dominique was not concerned with her baby's father, nor was she worried that anyone would threaten her son. She named Mandela for the real Nelson, and for a vague period of time that represented, in her mind, the best qualities a young man could have— strength, wisdom, smart power and patience in struggle. She named him for the time of Public Enemy videos and black fist air bush tees on 125th Street, before the Starbucks descended on the strip and the African Mart shopping center disappeared.

Back when Dominique began to dream of having babies, this moment seemed to her to be a permanent mark history's timeline. At sixteen, she had thought that, with a name like Mandela, her son, like the era of red, black and green in which she grew up, would be respected, formidable, difficult for the world to deny and impossible for it to forget. She did not mention to anyone her profound disappointment when she noticed the colors of that time beginning to fade. When the African vendors on 125th Street were swept from the sidewalk and piled into a dirty green tent on Lenox Avenue, she only sighed with Yunnique and shook her head. And when the H.M.V. music store and the Modell's Sporting Goods cropped up shiny and sleek in the vendors' place and her girls got ready to shop, Dominique went along, folding the rows of tables of bootleg tapes that had once lined the street into her memory.

She may have gone wrong with Mandela's name, but she would be sure with Adale. Adale was not, Dominique knew, the name of a man whose life could evaporate into history's stale air once the drama of his struggle subsided. Nor was it inspired by a time, which, she now understood, could be buried under the new and forgotten. Adale was not a name any of her friends had heard of, though they all agreed it was cute. Dominique had discovered her daughter's name early one morning shortly after Mandela was born. That night, he woke the entire house crying, and once she and her mother had quieted him and put him down again, Dominique was unable to sleep. There was little to watch on television, and so she found herself watching a bushy-haired white man on a charity infomercial, pleading into the camera, his eyes twinkling as thought hey contained fragments of falling stars. He slogged through moats of brown skin and garbage in a place filled impossibly with sun, the camera zooming in now and then on a pair of milk-pool eyes or a row of porcelain teeth. Speaking earnestly, a frail brown child dangling over his shoulder, the man urged the camera to send money to one of these children, the beautiful, starving children of Adale, Somalia.

Dominique hadn't known a lot about Africa, except that it was the smallest unit of place to which her lineage could be traced, and that it was not small enough for that to mean much. The idea of Africa felt especially vague now that its colors and sounds were so scarce on the streets of Harlem. But she remembered Somalia. She remembered hearing about that place everywhere years ago—seeing its name typed on the front covers of newspapers, hearing it come through the mouth of Mr. Collins, the junior high school math teacher, who had talked about the fighting there with more emotion than she had thought white math teachers could to muster for anything. Seeing all these years later that this place was still important, still calling the world's attention even in the dusty late hours of the morning, had struck Dominique. She couldn't send any money, having just had a baby for a useless man, having left school for the baby, and not yet having found a job. But still, she took note. She wrote the name in her round bubble lettering on a piece of marble notebook paper. The paper was lost within a year, but neither the name nor its spelling escaped her.

By the second Sunday of the year, the number had climbed to 158,000. An anchorwoman with golden-brown hair sat stiffly at her desk while, in a box over her shoulder, houses were swept away in white foam. Her elbows flapped awkwardly at her sides as she said the number in a low, unsteady voice, the t-s-word spilling from her lips again.

"Mama, that's how a snapper looks," Mandela said, looking up at Dominique from the table, one of Mrs. Potter's drug company pens in his hand. "Like that lady." He pressed the button on the back of the pen, tapping his feet against a box on the floor along with the clicking sound.

"Ssht, Mandela, I'm trying to listen," she said quickly. Then, looking at the boy, she added: "Go wash your hands. I'ma start breakfast."

Standing among the cardboard boxes in the near-empty pantry, she opened the glass canister where the rice had been kept and tried to imagine 158,000 grains. The ten pound bag of oatmeal she had bought from work for only five dollars (with coupon savings and her employee discount) had lasted almost a month, and would have lasted twice as long, she reminded herself, had the news not so distracted her from feeding her son. But now only powder and scattered oats remained at the bottom of the limp plastic bag. No where near 158,000. Not even enough for one last bowl.

She called up the stairs after Mandela to tell him that she was going to the store, to listen to Pop-Pop and finish packing his room while she was gone. She turned off the television, thought about it, then turned it back on again and left.

A young white couple had just bought the brownstone next door, which was once a crack house. Growing up, Dominique had had a brief friendship with a girl whose mother stayed there off-and-on. One time she had slipped into the building with the girl without her parents noticing, and had spent an afternoon smoking cigarettes in the dusty, wallpapered kitchen, listening to two women addicts tell stories about their lives. Now the building was a swarm of construction workers, cinderblocks, and massive trash bags hurled into a dumpster. The couple had moved into the upper floors just before Christmas, and already they'd laid their huge, desiccated evergreen across the seam of the pavement that bordered the Potters' home. Dominique lifted her leg high to step over the trunk, clearing the sidewalk that still belonged, she reminded herself, to her family.

The movement on the street was sparse and slow. Dominique imagined it was because most people were warm at home watching the news, but she wasn't sure. As she walked toward the Pathmark, a bare-legged blonde woman in a short skirt and knee-high boots walked toward her, holding a pair of expensive-looking black sunglasses limply in her hand. When she was within a few feet of Dominique, the woman turned her head and gave an open-mouthed half-smile, as though she were about to say something but realized at the last minute she had nothing to say. Dominique had seen this expression often on these new faces over the past few years, but she had never figured out how to read it. She parted her lips in response and felt only cool air in the sides of her mouth as the woman's body cut the breeze in swift passing.

Cold air smacking her teeth, Dominique thought of Adale, and of the place she would think have to think of as home. She imagined her baby girl born into a buildingless place of cars and malls and dark trees whose bushy green tops crowded the sky. There would be no music on the streets, no subways or corner stores. What there would be was a thick sun like in the commercial. There would be mud, grass, her and her family out there, somewhere, in a short two-bedroom house, but with heat, the rent paid, more and better food to eat. It could be alright for Adale to grow up someplace like that, Dominique practiced telling herself. She wouldn't know home like Dominique had known it, but she also wouldn't have to watch it swept away. It could be that was the best thing in the end.

Clusters of church women moved down Broadway in low, clinking heels, past the police barricades and heaps of renovation lumber that lined some of the blocks. At the corners, they gathered, piling into town car cabs on their way to Sunday service. Dominique recognized some of the women in one group from her mother's church. She paused and gave a dutiful smile as she approached, just as the women piled into a maroon Lincoln. One woman in a plush fur coat rolled down the back window and stuck her hand out into the air, shaking her fingers in a flutter to halt Dominique in front of the new GNC Nutrition Store.

"Hey, baby!" Her lips were painted a bright, festive red. She gave Dominique a wide smile from the cavern of the cab.

"Hi." Dominique smiled benignly again and rested her hand on her belly. She couldn't remember the woman's name, and she was sure the woman didn't remember hers, but it didn't matter. She was a woman from the church, Dominique was Mrs. Potter's daughter, and that was that. This easy anonymity was comforting. "How you doin' this mornin'?"

"Fine, sugar, don't pay to complain." The car

bobbed as someone in the back seat rustled their impatience. The woman smiled and pointed to Dominique's stomach. "When you due?"

"Three-and-a-half weeks." Now a real smile spread on Dominique's face, her skin warming in the cold. "Hopefully she'll be a Valentine's baby."

"Well, God bless you!" The cab began to roll forward. "Tell your mother I said happy New Year! Tell her make sure she call me fore y'all go upstate. My sister's up there—Ella, you remember, used to work at the World Trade. She been up there a year now. Say the quiet gets to her, but leas' she can pay the rent easy. Told me she taken to gardening. Turnips, of all the things." She sighed. "Anyway, tell your mama we'll miss her. This place is changing faster than I-don't-know what. But I wish y'all the best. Specially that little one!" She pointed to Dominique's belly again. Then she gave a final smile and the window screeched up into its groove as the car sped ahead.

For several months, there had been a huge mass of scaffolding and a wall of cinderblock piles on the corner of 145th Street, where the Rodriguez 99-Cent Store had once been. Some said a new Radio Shack would open there soon; others insisted it would be a CVS or a Walgreen's—the kind of pricier drugstore chain you used to only find downtown. A small crowd was gathering under the scaffolding now, slim figures in matching blue baseball caps and vests unfolding tables and hauling cardboard boxes out of an open van parked on the corner. The neighborhood people passing slowed down to watch. Dominique passed the scene with numb disinterest. She wasn't sure what the vests and tables were about, but the scaffolding meant what it always did—a change that would come too late for her to see it. She felt the baby kick.

At the Pathmark, Dominique said hello to the bag check man and a few of the stockers. The Pathmark had opened two years ago, replacing the tiny, run-down C-Town, which sagged with dull produce and dented cans. For Dominique, the Pathmark was a pleasure, even on her day off. It was like its own small world of nourishment and exchange—there was the cheese section, full of gloved professionals and pea-coated students nibbling free samples, and the bakery corner, with church women squeezing loaves of bread and fathers ordering birthday cakes for their sons. She made a lap around the market's crowded periphery, surveying all the things she had never tasted—the different types of yogurt and milk, the brightly-colored dips and sauces chilling coolly on their shelves. Fruits whose bright reds and purples seemed to wink from their bins, surprising her every time.

Her back began to ache a little as she waived to the young Dominican boy who worked the butcher section and rounded the corner of the cereal aisle. The ten-pound oatmeal was no longer on sale, she discovered, stooping to the family-size packages on the bottom shelf. She counted the days until the family would leave New York, multiplied by two to accommodate the burnt pots, and slid a four pound cardboard canister off of the middle shelf instead.

The only male cashier at the store was a young Kenyan man named Reginald, with skin the color of a ripe cherry. He was working her register today, and he smiled as she approached.

"Beautiful," he said. "What are you doing here on Sunday?"

Dominique shrugged and smiled limply. "I gotta make breakfast," she said, and put the canister on the shiny black conveyer belt. "Plus I had to check up on my register." She smiled again. She liked talking to him. His accent reminded her of the way 125th Street used to sound, its vowels stuffed with cotton and its consonants both sharp and blunt like old nails. She waited for him to talk some more.

"When will it be time for baby number two?" He smiled back and passed the oatmeal over the scanner. "That one is gonna be another boy. Only boys sit low like that."

"No," Dominique shook her head and ran a hand over the tabloid display. "It's a girl. She's due February. Valentine's."

"Oh, you know already, heh?" He tilted his head and looked at her stomach. "So what are you gonna name her?"

"Adale." Dominique felt warmth on her face again as she handed him her employee ID.

A smile lit his cheeks and he chuckled. "Oh, like in Africa, heh? What do you know about Adale? Have you ever been to Somalia?"

Dominique shook her head no. "I seen it on TV," she said. "And in the papers a long time ago. You been there? Is it pretty?"

He scanned her card and his smile faded. "You know, it's very bad over there right now. No water for so long, and then this."

Of all the words she'd heard the newscasters say in all her hours of tsunami news-watching, no one had mentioned Somalia, and she couldn't remember hearing anything about Africa at all. It was not excitement, of course, Dominique would say she felt when she heard that Somalia had been affected. What welled in her stomach as he told her about the devastation there was an ache, for sure. But whipped into the ache was a tiny reassurance—a grain of something like pride that made her want to smile and hide her face at once. Listening to him, she grew surer and surer that Adale's name was right. It was a name that would not be forgotten; it would be part of the tickertape of numbers that had escalated all these days on the television screen.

She tried to imagine the piles of wrecked fishing boats he described laying along the beaches of Adale. She pictured the roads and wells he said had vanished into water after four years of sand-scratching draught. She felt her belly stir, felt it move in the direction of this man's story. The name would appear, she was sure, on the screen beside the pug-necked reporters. It would be written in whatever book as part of this undeniable time in history—the catastrophe and the compassion and the overcoming and the relief, all documented alongside her daughter's name, right there. This was a moment that mattered, Adale was a place that mattered, and so her daughter would matter too.

By the time she left the store, the air on the street had settled into a deeper chill and a flatter shade of gray. She climbed 145th Street as quickly as she could, the pain still pinching her back and now creeping outward and grabbing around her waist and shoulders. The spattering of people in front of the would-be-Walgreen's had grown to twenty or so, and now she saw two white men on ladders struggling to attach a sign printed TSUNAMI RELIEF over the building's skeletal awning. Dominique approached, the dull pain pulsing over her hips as she stepped up onto the curb.

"Those children are so beautiful," she heard a woman say as she got closer. Two women stood in front of her, one blonde and one with brown hair that fell at her neck in a bump. They had their backs to her, and their purses rested casually on the folding table. At the table, two men and a woman sat in their blue vests and caps, peering over cardboard boxes stuffed with white envelopes and two large water jugs, each filled a few inches high with bills and change. Dominique had $6.51 in her wallet, and not much more at home.

The brown-haired woman pulled the cap from a shiny burgundy-and-gold pen and began to scribble on her checkbook.

"Oh, I know. Absolutely gorgeous," the other woman said. She dug into a brown-roped purse Dominique recognized as a Louis Vuitton. "Those exotic babies are stunning. You just want to eat them up, poor things."

Dominique said nothing to the women, but when she got to the table, she sat her oatmeal beside plastic jug with a thud. "I want to make a donation for Adale," she said. The man behind the table looked up at her and smiled warmly, his pale skin flushing as a breeze hit. "Hello," he said, as though he hadn't heard her. "Thanks for making a donation. Would you like an envelope, or will you be donating cash?"

"Cash." Dominique smiled back and opened her wallet. "For Adale."

"I'm sorry?"

"Somalia." She said, tired. She rested her hand on her belly. "I'm donating money for Somalia."

"I'm sorry, miss," he said. "We're only collecting for tsunami relief." When she explained that she understood that, and that she wanted to give money to tsunami victims in Somalia, he pressed his gloveless hands to his cheeks and told her that they would not be able to send donations to any specific country—that the money they raised would go to an organization whose name she recognized and who, he assured her with soft eyes, would provide aid for the countries that needed it most.

She gave him a polite thank-you, and asked for an envelope. He told her that the envelopes were for check donations only, and she told him that she understood that and would like an envelope anyway, and a piece of paper as well. Then she slid a pen and clipboard off of the table, and wrote "Adale" in dark letters, as beautifully, she hoped, as the first time she wrote it. She slid the paper neatly into the envelope, the letters facing front, and stuffed her money—the bills, the quarters, and even the penny—behind it.

As she turned away from the table, leaving the envelope in the man's hands, Dominique heard the women talking.

"Somalia?" The Vuitton woman's hands had disappeared into the pockets of her long gray coat.

"Yeah, I heard someone say there was a little damage to the coast of Africa, too." The brown-haired woman looked at Dominique as she pushed by.

"Only 300 people died there, you know," the woman said loudly. Dominique wasn't sure if she was talking to her, but she felt the words hit hard.

She parted her lips to say something, but the women gusted away before she figured out what. Watching them disappear into the new Bank of America whose awning glowed red, white, and blue up the street, Dominique considered this number: 300. It was a number she could more comfortably understand. She imagined the three hundred dollars she would find in her last pay check from her job—the only one she'd had in this place where she had lived her life and had her first child. She thought of the three hundred minutes she had spent in labor with Mandela, and the many cycles of three hundred sixty five days she had passed thinking of her children, planning for them and giving them as much as she could of what she thought they might need in the world. The plastic bag swung from her hands and knocked against her knees as she walked the long blocks back to the house, hoping that her mother and father would join them this morning for breakfast, and that Mandela had packed the last of his books.

Friday, Field Trip Day

The little boy is disgusted by the monkeys, but adores the lions the way his classmates adore their big brothers and young uncles. They are slow and deliberate, they cannot be bothered by the bugs that gather on their manes and tails. They swat them away in a rhythm, and the boy tries to grasp it—a swat, a pause, a swat-swat, pause again. It reminds him of the hands of his mother's watch. At home, he has tried to understand the numbers, to predict what they will do, but always they confuse him. His father has given him a toy watch to practice with, and he tries, but he always gives up, frustrated. The lions, the thinks, have mastered time. They yawn, they stop, they walk, they rest. They look in the direction they are headed, to the rock wall, to the water well, to who knows where.

The biggest lion passes the through boy's shadow behind the bars of the cage. Two paws through his outstretched arm, the mane sliding into his shoulder. The shadows merge, and for a second, he is a boy with a lion across his chest. Then, paws out of his ribcage, a tail brushing through his left hand, past his little blue camera, the little toy watch, a gift from his father.

Judith, his mother, is standing in front of the kitchen sink, drying her own mother's china with a tea towel. She feels she has not seen or touched any of these things—her mother, the china, the kitchen sink—in ages. She rubs the plate hard, fast, her hair bucking and swaying from her head as her back and shoulders move. If the boy were here, he might think she was angry. At the dishes? At his father? But she is thinking about her son this afternoon, knowing deeply and quietly his wish to be a lion, admiring that quality in him, a result of her influence. She is wondering what she will tell him when she sees him today, how she will explain what has happened—what is happening—why she is home. Quietly, she is worrying about the moment when he discovers, much later, she hopes, that boys don't grow up to be lions after all.

She is the one who has given him his best traits, she thinks as she rotates the dish against the towel. Though her husband's music has helped out some—mainly jingles for local diners and small hardware chains—she is the one who supplied the natural creative talent. She is the one who nurtures his imagination, who beams and coos over the paintings and drawings, who has them framed and hangs them next to the Degas prints. Her husband has contributed mostly time. To her, this is a valuable contribution, a good thing for a father to give a son. She has been glad about their life.

Most days around this time, she is at her desk or at a meeting, and for a minute she imagines what the two of them are doing, father and son. Soon her husband would be picking the child up, since it's Friday—their day to "hang," her husband would say.

Any other day, he would spend the early afternoon "jamming" with his friends, and then pick the boy up from after-school. They would go home, have a snack, and he would put dinner on. Then he would retreat to his "studio," the small shed off the side of the kitchen, and work on his songs. He would start the songs and stop them over and over, she imagined, emerging absently three or four times throughout the evening. First, he would take a break check the food, to stir it, to help a little with homework. Then, once she arrived home and the food was done, he would come out again to serve it and eat too much, to wash the dishes and eat some more. He would appear once again, perhaps, to go to the bathroom a few hours later; and, finally, he would emerge at three or four in the morning time to drag his weight up the stairs and heave himself into bed beside her, sometimes still humming whatever song he'd been writing.

These days it's a love song. When the songs are about love, she finds, this is when she is least in love with him. She cannot resist the urge to imagine that he is singing about someone else. The "storm of sand that steals my rain" could not be her. This is someone smaller, with wider eyes and better cheekbones, someone who will look at him in ways that she no longer can. And even though he seems to her to be too lazy for an affair—and even though, truly, he has never seemed to her to be the type, which is part of why she married him—still, hearing his love songs, she resents him.

But when the songs are about other things—tuna subs and steam cleaning services—she is inspired to love him well. He would think, for sure, that this is because the jingles bring money to the house and make him seem responsible, but that's not it. She feels these jingles show his true talent. He is not an artist, she feels, so much as a riddler. His poetry is unremarkable, but his ability to arrange collections of words and concepts into short snippets of song—Carpet Hut, Plankton Street, "Our staff is well-trained and helpful!" "We won't be undersold!"— astounds her. During these times, when there are jingles, she is pleased with the balance they have established; his gigs, her talent, her career, his work, their house, their marriage, their life, their son.

These days it is a love song, but even so there was a moment of almost-tenderness this morning. She woke up and thought for sure that she was right, that he was off sleeping with someone else, because he was not in the bed. She had not heard him lumbering up the stairs at dawn, she had not felt him sink into the mattress beside her, causing her to roll back slightly in her sleep as happened most nights. There was no smell of anything cooking in the kitchen when she woke up, and she did not hear him in the bathroom. He was with his love, his muse, she decided, wild with fantasy. She would divorce him right away. Then when she saw the light on in the shed on her way out of the house, she was relieved. She felt, for a second, an urge to pop her head into the shed door like a movie wife or a young girlfriend, to tell him to have a good day, remind him that she would be home late, perhaps even blow him a kiss. But then she saw that the boy was almost late for school, and she for work, and so the moment passed.

The boy is one of only two or three in his class

whose fathers come to pick them up after school. It is mostly nannies from other countries, or babysitters. His father is a musician, he comes to pick him up every day from after-school. Some days, like today, Friday, field trip day, Dad will come early. And because Dad will come, the boy will not have to go to after-school, where they feed him stale oatmeal cookies that turn to powder in his mouth, and where they do not let him do what he wants to do. There are no kids from his class in after-school. There are only larger kids that sweat a lot and talk loud all the time. At after-school, they make them do activities, uninteresting things like tying cups together with yarn and pretending it makes a telephone. They will not let him sit and draw. They make him do activities he hates forever. Time goes so slow it becomes heavy on him. He gets tired and he begins to feel that if he does not do something interesting, his skin will erupt into an itch. This is one of the things he does not say to anyone. He does not know the words, and even if he did, he is not sure he would say them.

There are a lot of things he doesn't explain to anyone. He likes drawing mainly because he likes to hold the crayons between his pointer finger and his thumb, likes to peel away the tan-and-black, aqua-and-black, magenta-and-black paper in rivulets and press his nails into the wax. It gives him a satisfaction he cannot name, one that he gets he-can't-think-where else. Maybe from pressing his tongue against his gums when he has a loose tooth, or from biting the inside of his cheek lightly, then stopping for a while and biting some more. These are the greatest satisfactions of his life, though he can't say why. When he tries to explain them to his parents or cousins, it does not work. They give him a tilted eyebrow look for a second, then returned to whatever they were doing. From their looks, he learns that these are private feelings, feelings that could not be explained, not really, feelings that maybe should not be explained, even if he did learn the words.

He wonders if lions have these feelings, the private, important ones that no one understands. He is tempted to ask the teacher, but he refrains. The class is moving toward the picnic tables—the teacher says it's time for lunch. He feels it is too early. He has just eaten breakfast not so long ago in the car with his mother, and he would rather stand here against the hot metal railing and think about the lions. But remembering the good ham sandwich his father packed for him, he decides it is okay that the time has come to eat.

Later, many years later in life, there would be moments when time was flattened into a thin wisp, a passing scent, a question unasked in a split-second decision, and then lost forever. There would be times when, standing before the toilet after a long day spent working and needing to pee, the pleasure of release would be so great, so freeing, that he would have to wonder whether time had passed at all, or had it all been dreamt up? Was he a grown man come home dogged from work, or was he, in actuality, a seven-year-old boy urinating in his sleep?

By middle age, the questions would take on new shapes and tones. Simple questions like *Can a boy become a lion?* would become frantic and imploring, and might cause him to slam tables in arguments with women or fall asleep, drunk, a lit cigarette in his hand. And large questions like *What is love* would fade slowly into the light of various dawns until they had simply disappeared, leaving only a faint imprint on his face, like fog on an attic window.

But for now, time was an unfathomable expanse drawn in bold colors: green and brown for trees, brown for dirt, brown for the hair of his mother and his father and his cousins and himself. Red for apples and farmhouses, blue for water and skies. Time held all these things just out of his reach, just beyond his understanding of the numbers on the clocks that could never go past a certain point, never to 67, their house number, or 92, the number of their road. Time did hold promises, though. It promised that one day soon would be his birthday, and that eventually he would be able to tie his shoes the real way, without having to loop each lace first into bunny ears and then knot them together.

It promised that all these things he felt for the lions, he would one day become, that that was why he felt these things in the first place. He would one day walk high and tall on his two legs, pass between the shadows and keep his eyes forward, focused on something important only he needed to know. Time promised that soon the class would pile onto the bus where he would sit next to fat Jordan Richards and talk about television shows. Time promised that they would return to the classroom, that it would smell the same way it smelled when they left, like oatmeal and play dough, and that before long his father would come to pick him up and take him home. He would not have to go to after-school today. They would stop for Chinese food on the way to the house, since today was Friday, trip day, his mother's late night at work.

She has never liked her husband's friends. She runs hot water in the basin and squeezes the dish soap too hard. Half the liquid shoots into the water and a mound of bubbles spring up almost instantly. She has never liked them. They are all fat, all irresponsible. None of them have changed since college. None of them have given up their addictions, none have figured out how to provide for anyone as well as her husband has. They should look to him as a role model, she thinks, but they don't. They see him as a buddy, because they are still in the habit of having "buddies." They call him in the afternoon to "jam," to "play," but really just to hang out, eat pizza and drink beer. When they can't reach him, they call her, though she and he are rarely together—she works.

The one friend, Billy, called her four or five times this morning. It was a busy morning. She did not pick up the phone. She did not have time to check her messages until lunch. By 12:10 she was in the car, on the phone, driving, dialing, moving dizzily toward home. She had found it hard to hold the phone, she remembers now, gripping a clean soup bowl and dunking it firmly into the soapy water. She had had a hard time seeing the numbers on the phone, knowing who to dial. She had had trouble remembering how to press the buttons with her fingers and release the gas with her foot at the same time.

But somehow, she had found herself on the phone

with Billy, who told her things she hadn't understood then and cannot remember now—not well enough—now that she is home with the bubbles and the running water and the china that refuses to get clean. So she will wash these dishes again, and she will think. She will remember her mother's advice on how to clean good china. She will remember whose number to call. She will remember Billy's messages this morning, and she will think, she will think, she will think about what to tell her son.

Nine-something AM, just after the start of her first meeting, Billy: *Wondering where he was, they had to pitch an idea to a client, he was late. Call back.* Closer to ten, Billy: *Jude, hey, hoping nothing's wrong, something something. Call back.* Some time later, a message, or maybe many, Billy: *Jude, uh, don't have your work number, at the house, listen... uhh.* This she remembers. She remembers the length of his stammer, the porousness and uncertainty of his breath: *Jude, you gotta come, call, pick up, shit.*

He always said he would have a heart attack. It was a pun to him. By this he meant that his big, animal heart would one day snap out of his control and attack him for all the love he made it dole out, which he felt was largely unreciprocated. This love, he said, left holes in his heart that would germinate little heart armies, which would eventually grow to overthrow him. He would laugh about it, good and hard from the gut. She would tell him to stop smoking, stop drinking, stop gaining weight.

But she cannot think too much about these things, because she will drop the dishes, or she will miss spots of grease and they will not be clean, and then she will have to wash them again. People will be coming over soon, some people, she will call them. And she will need to serve them on clean plates. She will need to run the water, she will need to scrub, to rinse, to wash, to dry, to soap up. To think of what to say to her son. She has to wash the dishes and she has to think, and so she does not have to remember what else Billy said, who Billy is, what she saw when she turned the corner and found her door, her front door, looking so strange with a man-shaped bag rolling out of it that she wondered if she was on the right street, if this was her house after all. She does not have to remember the date, she does not have to remember the time, she only has to think, to think, just for a moment.

The black nannies have all come. The mothers have all come with their big smiles and their hugs. The fathers have come, but not his. The after-school children have already gone down to the basement to be fed powdery cookies and juice from a can. The boy sits on the bench in the office while they call his mother at work. He tells them to call his father, that sometimes when his mother is at work she does not get to answer the phone. They call more people, someone, he doesn't know who.

The big black clock in the office is moving to a rhythm, and if he pays attention, he feels he can move with it. He can click his tongue or blink his eyes or bite his teeth along with the two black hands. He can predict where it will be in three bites, four. He remembers his multiplication tables, thinks about the fives. Maybe his mother will come instead, he thinks. Maybe she will surprise him and cook dinner instead of take-out. He would rather take-out, but she is a better cook than Dad, at least. Sometimes he wishes she were a musician instead of Dad. When she cooks, her meat is soft and juicy and easy to chew, and he even likes the taste of her broccoli when he dips it in the juice from the steak. But in the office the secretary tells someone else he will have to go down to after-school. He is not surprised, but he is something else, something numb he cannot name. They will come, they will hold his hand and walk him down to the basement. He would rather do almost anything else.

He would rather sit and learn this clock. He would rather rub his fingers along the ridges of the wood bench until his father arrives. He would rather not have to hold the hand of the secretary or some other person, a hand that will be huge and strange and cold and sweaty. He would rather not have that hand lead him to a place he suddenly hates more than anything in the world.

He looks out the door down the long, muraled hallway to the stairwell. There are paintings of children laughing on these walls, different colors of skin and shirts. There are people playing, holding their arms out, smiling toward him at the center of the hallway. But he walks straight, looking at the stairs. He thinks about putting his hands in his pocket so no one will come and grab them, but instead he keeps them at his side. He walks not slow, but not fast, counting his steps, his own faultless rhythm. No matter the activity, he decides, no matter the puzzle-making or puppet show, he will find a way to draw. He walks straight and thinks of the things.

Ruídos

"Nunca he tenido miedo," Aldóvar said, his voice curling with his cigarette smoke past the dusty saxophone beside him, disappearing into the room. He ran his fingers over the red wine stain that had spread, thick and sticky, across the dining room table. He could feel the woman's eyes on him, teeming, he was sure, with pity. He didn't need to look at her—just imagining the look on her face warmed him. He examined the crescents of dirt under his nails, tapped hard on the cigarette and said it again: *I have never been afraid. I have never had fear.* But she had already left the room.

Aldóvar had been sitting this way, in this corner of the dining room, in this specific marinade of beer and smoke and what he felt was sad wisdom for ten days straight now—since the morning of his thirty-fifth birthday, when he awoke to find that Patrick had gone to work, taken the car, and left him with nothing more than a birthday note, in which he promised at once to be back soon and to stay gone forever. Since then, Aldóvar had gotten up only a handful of times. He rose once daily to use the bathroom. On Tuesday, he had gone to the living room for the box where the marijuana was kept. On Thursday, he went to the little studio room to get his alto saxophone so that it could sit beside him and remind him of his beauty and all the ways he'd failed. On Saturday night, the dining room light had died, and he got up to pull the window shade a little so he could re-read the note in the light from the alley next door. Only today had he gone outside— first to the deli on 73rd and York for a pack of Camels and some rolling papers, then to the East River, where he walked slow and talked to the pigeons until he found what he was looking for, sitting on a bench in old sneakers and a red skirt.

Now back home, with the woman there, watching, breathing, filling the space with him, he could read Patrick's note once again. The note had been ten notes, a new note every time Aldóvar brought it to his face to squint at it under the back alley light. Ten days ago, it was a note about his birthday, a happy one, which Patrick would help him celebrate when he returned from the school, carrying a butterscotch cake. The note had said several things since then—things about his mother, his people, his home in Chile. Things about his thinning body and his habits, this attempt at a home here on the Upper East Side. By today, the tenth day, the note told him to mill about, to go out, to mourn and cry to someone else. All this in the last line, in the long indent, the short, indifferent dash where love should have been: "—Patrick."

Pots rattled in the kitchen and a light came on. "Eso no puede ser, mi alma," she said from down the hall. *Fear isn't optional in life. In memory, maybe, but that's it.*

The smell of food began to spread through the

house—meats with comino and achiote, soups that smelled like things his grandmother said her grandmother used to make.

"No me digas nada de la vida. No me conoces." Aldóvar started up from his corner, intending to gallop into the kitchen and tell this woman something about life and memory and the respect of the two. *Don't tell me about life. You don't know me.* But he burned himself with the cigarette he'd forgotten was in his hand, and rolled back into his corner, cursing.

She chuckled from the doorway. "Te quemaste, ¿eh, ancianito?" *You burned yourself, huh, old man? Little ancient man?*

He heard her thighs clap together as she walked away from him, down the hall, pausing every few steps to crack a door open and look in. Finally, he heard her step into the bathroom at the end of the hall and turn the water on. Then she was back, holding a wad of toilet paper, a stick of butter, and Patrick's rosewater jug.

"El me piensa infante," he said. "Tu tambien, a lo mejor. No saben na." *He thinks I'm a child. A pretty brown boy to play with and take care of. You think the same, but I disgust you, too. You both think I should be a man. Neither of you knows anything.*

One hand on the table top, she knelt by him and dabbed his palm, first with the butter, then with the rosewater and tissue. He felt her, he smelled her, and he thought he could find his mother speaking to him through this woman's lips. If he closed his eyes, he thought, these breasts brushing his shoulders and these fingers pressed on his hand could become the body of his ex-wife in Santiago, his first girlfriend in Isla

Negra, all the roundness and softness of the lives he had lived before.

"¿Qué sería mi vida sín tí?" He said to her, dizzily. *What would my life be without you?*

She fingered the saxophone. *Don't talk to me about life. You don't know me.*

The children blew and banged on instruments all week, but Patrick did not mind. The sounds were horrid, airy, riotous, but he didn't wince. They'd begun, this afternoon, to throw things at each other, and Patrick was calmer than he had ever known himself to be. He took them aside individually and explained, for what it was worth, that instruments, like people, were to be respected, and that shoving or hitting either was unacceptable. He doled out time-outs and trips to the principal's office liberally but without malice. Palmer and Jackson told him in the lounge that he looked good, like a new man, they said, and they asked if he'd lost weight. On the first day after he left Aldo, Richards, the only other male teacher in the school—a science teacher, also gay—touched his shoulder and complimented him on his suit. It was a navy pinstripe which he had forgotten entirely until ten days ago, when he showed up, dazed, at his ex-wife's house, a butterscotch cake in tow.

"Rhon," he had said, and she opened the door and hugged him. She asked about Aldo, about their music and their apartment. He tried, at first, to tell her that things were fine, but by evening he had lost all his energy and could not explain his shattered face away. They cut the cake and spent the evening in the house where he had lived his last life, on the couch where she had helped him mourn his mother's death, at the table where he had told her, over toast and eggs, that he needed a divorce. And now, years later, she listened to him as he explained Aldo's mystery, the beauty of his sadness and his confusion, the terrible weight of his pain. He told her how hard it was to make music after work every day when Aldo had not played a note in months, how he drove around the block twice or three times each afternoon to delay coming home to a man that had not lived a second of life since he left him. Rhonda had worked through three slices of cake while listening, easing off bites of white sponge and smears of soft yellow cream with the edge of her fork and murmuring "yeah, *mmhm*," her eyes locked on his as he talked. He had stayed with her since, talking and eating, and had not yet had to ask how life was treating her.

That first evening, he found his old suits, and was reminded of a past version of himself, one whose primary pursuit in life was to convince the world he was a certain kind of man. He wore the charcoal gray suit to school the next day, then some black ones and a slate gray stripe. There were ties, too, responsible ones with just enough flare to say, *"And I have personality, too."* He had waived to old neighbors all week as he picked up the paper, smiled at them as he pulled into the driveway each evening. He had cooked for Rhonda twice—stuffed artichokes and risotto with basil on Friday, apple French toast with mixed berries and crème fraiche for Sunday brunch. She had come home from work as she used to, with bottles of wine and CDs by new artists her company had discovered. Each night, they would peel the cellophane off of the cases and look at the promo photos—a Tunisian-Swiss folksinger, a Franco-American electro band—and she would say which ones she thought had promise, which seemed too naïve or too indulgent for their own good. They judged together. They comforted each other. They ate and drank and laughed like young lovers, like life-long friends.

There had even been moments when she reminded him of Aldo—Aldo in the early days, four-and-a-half years ago, when his English was bare and essential, forcing him to rely mostly on more precise means of communication. These days with Rhon reminded Patrick of the time when he was a young man, married to a beautiful young woman executive, growing more and more willing each day to throw his life away for this person—another man—who made languages with his eyes and vows with his music. In a rented basement studio, they had played—first for each other, then with each other, first lightly and then not lightly at all—for nearly a year. They had played in a band together, and their first times touching happened late in the evenings, after the other band members had left, but soon they began to arrange to meet early in the afternoons, before the others arrived. Eventually there were hotel rooms, bed and breakfasts, and finally, the apartment on 73rd.

"Patrick, it's going to happen, ok?" Aldo had said many times after hours of playing and pulling and pressing together, stretched and sweaty. "Music, I mean. We have to make it. I'm telling you."

"Ok, Aldo," he had responded, noticing only his fingers in Aldo's long black hair, Aldo's soft, stubbly cheek in his palm, the pulse of them both, pleading beneath their skins to be kissed and touched some more.

These things Patrick remembered in Rhonda's house no longer existed in the apartment on York. These good memories had been forgotten, like his suits and his pride and his patience, under heaps of Aldo—his fallen dreams, his broken heart, his eyes whose precision and eloquence had cracked and left nothing but water.

Suited up and driving back to a home that had seen light all day, and to a person who had lived, Patrick resolved not to go back. He had known it all along, he decided. Eleven nights ago when he circled the block three times and entered the apartment to find Aldo face down in his own vomit, a full ashtray smoking beside him on the dining room floor. And before that even, each day that passed without Aldóvar's *making it*. It seemed to Patrick that Aldo had devoted himself to proving it was all or nothing for him, that if he could not succeed he would be sure to fail. It was not surprising, Patrick resolved now. It was there from the beginning, all these years. It had taken him some time to see it, but as soon as he did, he acted—in his best interest and in Aldo's, too. He found all the words he could and he tried to say them, stuff them into the curves and lines of the note he had left on the dining room table:

Aldo,
I hope you feel better, and that your
birthday is good to you.
I cleaned up the mess. I'm going to work.
Money is in the cabinet.
Food in the fridge. Please eat.

— Patrick

"Pero, ¿por qué no me quiere jamás?" *But why doesn't love me anymore?*

But for Matilda, of course, there wasn't much to say. She did not know what was going on, really, except that this man was in love with another man, most likely a white man, who lived in a nice apartment and spoke good enough English, which he used to write what seemed like a fairly straightforward note, with a fairly straightforward message: goodbye.

But there was a lot of good food in the kitchen, and she had not eaten good food in a while—nothing better than wings from the Crown Fried Chicken on 86th or hard rice and green pea slop from the cafeteria at the hospital where she worked, a few blocks away from this apartment. She had not been to work in a while, had not really talked to anyone, about anything, in days. There was no reason why, at least none to speak of. There had been a man, and now there was not, and the only thing there was to say about him was that he was gone, leaving her to swim in the silence she'd become during their time together. He had been loud and she had been quiet, and she hadn't noticed it until it was too late. Now that he was gone, the quiet was all there was—quiet buzzing from the bathroom where he used to brush his teeth, quiet ringing from the sofa where he used to shout at basketball games, quiet clanging in the kitchen where he had slammed dishes and punched the wall, not often, but sometimes, while she stood there, mute. She felt menaced by the quiet now, in the sour way that comfort can menace. It was with her and it was in her—her throat and ears plugged with things unsaid.

So it was fine with her to have seen this man out

the corner of her eye, cursing at pigeons on the FDR Drive this morning. She clocked his type immediately—the expensive but dirty clothes, the fancy shoes left unlaced and run-over—he was a pampered drifter. Men like him—and weren't they all?—they always needed someone to take care of them. A bosomy mother, a sexy nurse, an audience for whatever elaborate show. She was too tired from the last man to offer much, but men like him never noticed those things. They wanted, and they usually received. But this one would have something to offer her. Men who needed to be taken care of usually were—more than taken care of, in fact, with plenty extra to go around. She could tell when she saw him that there would be food, maybe money, and who knew what else. At the very least, there would be sound.

"No sé, mi vida," she put his hand back in his lap and stood up. "¿Como puede ser?" *Why doesn't he love you? I don't know, my dear, my life. Look at you. What's not to love?*

His laughter broke into a mucusy cough.

"Bueno, amor, levántate. Vamos a comer." She held him now for the first time, pulling him up by his shoulders and leaning both their weights on a tall wooden chair. *Get up. We're going to eat.*

In her arms, his smell surprised her. It was not the simple compound of smoke, beer, and weed she had expected. There was a cinnamon smell, or maybe nutmeg, something that must belong to this white man—his soap, perhaps, or his shampoo. Had she noticed this smell on Aldóvar sooner, down by the water, she might have smiled at him. As it was, his sweet, sad face had only been enough to elicit a commanding "Hola, papi, how you doing today?"

"Bien, ¿y usted, señorita?" He had said, stumbling up to her bench with a cigarette in one hand and a paper bag in the other, the teal morning sky hanging heavy over his head. *Fine, and you, young lady?*

"Todo bien," she had answered. "Gozando del ruído." She leaned back on the bench with her legs straight in front of her, looking past him as the cars whipped the air. *Good, all good, enjoying the noise.*

This was exactly what she had been doing on that bench since the day before yesterday when the silence in her apartment began to beat on her ears. She had left that afternoon without her work uniform, without her tattered staff ID, without even five dollars, to go listen to the cars hum and the wind fly down the FDR. The man had not thought—or at least he had not said—that she was strange to be sitting there. He had not asked her why she so craved noise. He had not asked her to tell her story, to justify her restlessness or her effort to strangle it with sound.

By the time they had reached his apartment, she was sure he would expect her to sleep with him. This would not be the worst thing in the world, she had decided. She might do it. She had not been with a man in some time—the man who left had lost interest in that part of her months ago—and now the thought of sex brought to mind a set of huge, disfigured, subsuming sounds she'd almost forgotten. But when he pushed the door open and ushered her into the apartment, he had not so much as offered to take her jacket. He walked directly to the corner of the dining room and spilled down to the floor, amid a pile of Corona bottles, beside an ashtray, a box of weed, and a saxophone.

Matilda had often thought of being played like a musical instrument. She had imagined the feel of a bass player pushing deep against her g-spot, a guitarist who could pluck her clitoris like a knot of tight strings, the million tiny, cool notes a flautist might wrap around her neck. Sex with this man would not be a chore or mistake, she thought, looking at the brassy instrument. She had not yet imagined what a saxophone might be like.

"Hay vino en la nevera," he had said without looking at her. He licked a white paper and began to crumble clumps of weed into it. *There's wine in the fridge.*

Matilda was surprised to find that the wine in the refrigerator was a merlot. The well-stocked wine rack beside the pantry door indicated that someone around here knew not to chill red wine. Matilda was proud to know this, too. Still, she had liked her red wine cold since junior high school, when she discovered that the taste of cold cheap red wine was not entirely different from the taste of grape juice—not the sugary, purple bodega kind, but the real thing, bloody and bittersweet, from the gourmet stores on Madison Avenue. She had poured herself a glass and sat.

"Pues, ¿tu eres músico?" *So you're a musician?*

"Ah, linda, mejor dicho soy fracaso." Laughter. *Better put, I am a failure.*

"Pero eso te gusta, ¿no?" she said. *You seem to like that title.*

"Es el único que tengo. Me debe gustar." He rolled the joint, lit it, and took a pull. *I have to like it. It's all I got.*

Matilda had known men like this, hopeless

dreamers who bathed themselves in the wreckage of fantasy to keep from having to make anything out of real life. Her father had been one, and her brother, and the man who'd left was probably one as well, although that, too, she had failed to notice in time. These men were selfish, too selfish to live with, but also too selfish not to love, at least a little. The insistence of their misery was pitiful, almost comical, and beautiful at once. The key, she thought now, was to take what they could offer and give them *just* that little bit, just enough so that the giving cost her nothing, and perhaps even felt good. Perhaps that was the closest she would come to an equal exchange.

"Qué caballero eres," she said. "Que no compartes la hierba con tu compañera." She crossed her legs and leaned toward him. *What kind of gentleman are you, that you don't even share the herb with your lady friend?*

"Es que si fumamos juntos," he said, dabbing the joint against the ashtray, "tu te vas a enamorar de mí." He coughed. *If we smoke together, you'll fall in love with me. And I am a betrothed man.*

Matilda smiled and took the joint. She blew smoke in his face and asked him about his life. She pushed the tall dining room windows open and spread the drapes, flinging them against the wall with a *whack*. She made pepper steak and cabbage, the grease popping like rainstorms in the skillets, the boiling water a song of burbles and licks. She drank the wine and spilled it on the table, heard the glass crash to the floor, and laughed. She listened to him talk about his boyfriend, a white teacher who had left him drunk and sick and lonely on his birthday. Once he had slid the last of the cabbage into his mouth, she got up to take his plate. He grabbed her arm and held it.

"Tu eres la mujer de mis suenos, señorita," he said. *You are the woman of my dreams.*

Matilda put the plate on the table and lit a cigarette. *So you've fallen in love with me?*

"Claro."

So play me something.

He dragged the saxophone from the corner and began to play. Matilda heard his lungs' struggle, his breath like a smashed harmonica—all strain and no sound. But his fingers wrapped around the gold pads with more force than she had thought his body could muster. He pushed and pressed the instrument with a fierce diligence, and she began to believe that, eventually, something worth hearing would come out.

Patrick turned off of First Avenue, onto 73rd only once. He parked a few doors down and zipped up his jacket, keeping the car keys in his hand. He paid close attention to the look of the building—the low yellow lights of the lobby, the cracked marble floors in the hallways, the warm and faintly mildewy smell in the elevator, which the janitorial staff had never been able to defeat. He wanted to keep these things safe in his memory—because they were all memories now. Each floor that passed on the elevator, each number lit white as it climbed, was a step toward the end of this life and the beginning of the next one—a former life re-envisioned, refashioned and improved. The next life would be him and Rhon—friendly and comfortable—with good wine and a kitchen brimming with light. It would be his suits, the neighbors, a big airy home and weightless laughter. He would not take too much with him. He would not say too much of a goodbye.

The familiar groans of novice playing greeted him when the elevator doors opened on the eighth floor—an alto saxophone screeching a song he thought he might have heard once. But as Patrick walked toward his door, he heard the sounds easing down, tones becoming sturdier and more solid, notes clear as wind beginning to form. He turned his key in the lock and walked in to a place that he doubted, for a second, he had ever been before. Food and wine and an open window. Aldo playing the sax for a brown woman who sat on their dining room table with her legs crossed, smoking a cigarette. Her eyes were closed, and her head waved to the music.

But why doesn't he love me? became a song, and the men played it for her. One on the alto saxophone, one on the soprano. It was a battle of beauty, of blood and of hearts. Matilda felt her spirit running on the underside of her skin. The men would not stop. Their notes made love, told stories. Arguments ensued and stopped just short of violence. Promises were made, and kept, and broken, but the sound made no move to leave.

She sat with the saxophones, in the noisr of them, for what could have been hours, thinking about the rush of cars she had left this morning, the food she had just eaten, all the things she had heard today. She thought about these men—this stranger who had declared from a pit of ash and headache that he had never been afraid, and this other one who wrote clear notes and did, in fact, bring home a cinnamon smell, whose love and whose absence clearly terrified the first. She thought about her life, herself, all the things that were or could one day be. Humming a melody that both matched theirs and didn't, Matilda sipped her wine and listened as they talked.

The Anvil

My wild grace and I shift on my right hip. We perch there and tilt towards the airplane window, considering the possibility that I have swallowed an anvil in my daydream. Camera light on my cheeks, red liner sealing thickly my precisely drawn lips, I am sure of it. A rust-encrusted, black-barnacled anvil. And now that it has glubbed its way down my digestive tract, sliding to the seasick rhythm of my peristalsis, it sits, I'm sure, perched in my stomach, dangerously close to my womb. I run my tongue lightly over my teeth to clear away any nasty fuchsia smudges, angle my jaw and smile for the cameras.

I say this to no one, but: the Atlantic sky is looking thick and frothy, all sun and cloud, like banana pudding and lemon meringue. It compels me to dive in, reckless and open-mouthed, to swallow the air until I am full almost to bursting and raining myself. I am reminded of the time in the fourth grade when I ate the class gerbil. This, of course, was back when I was a large American civilian, and a carnivore.

Mr. Weiss, the nice baldheaded teacher, had charged me with pet duty for the afternoon. I had put up quite a dynamic protest, I remember, stomping my feet on the soft green carpet and sending him my sharpest look of malevolence, all to no avail. But I didn't eat Galileo out of spite. I did hate him for his alien grunts, which interrupted my dramatic readings in English class—a star on the rise, I was!—and for the cedar-and-feces funk he emitted, so offensive and impolite. Anyone who had cared to spend two minutes' thought on the matter could easily have deduced that I would never have intended to put the nasty rodent into my mouth, and that, in fact, I would sooner have taken a running leap over the George Washington Bridge, or run naked and barefoot through Marcus Garvey Park on Halloween night. But, of course, nobody thought about that. The fat girl ate the gerbil. It was quite a laugh.

The school called my mother, and she arrived more promptly than she had arrived for anything, ever. When I opened the door to the main office where I was to meet her, I saw Mr. Weiss shaking her hand gravely. She muttered long apologies through cascades of mascaraed tears, never bothering to ask me if, after having ingested an entire gerbil, I might need a glass of water or an x-ray. I was whisked onto the A train without so much as a word, and she succeeded in saying absolutely nothing to me until the following night before dinner, when, because my protruding stomach blocked the handle of the cabinet door, she was forced to ask me either to move or to pass her the cayenne pepper for her latest tabloid diet soup. Once this line of communiqué was reopened, I was subject to epics about the embarrassment she felt when her secretary (her secretary!) handed her the yellow message log paper stating that her only daughter had eaten the class pet. I was made to recall that day as the day my mother gave up on ever having grandkids, for what decent black man would marry a girl who would eat a gerbil? What assurance could he have that I would not eat the children and the microwave, too? I understand now, of course, that even my mother could not have known the heights of beauty and fame that I, then an unkempt, sloppy-figured Harlem girl, would one day reach. Still, the memory is painful, all the same.

I look away from the airplane window and notice a pregnant lady with a blonde pig-tail sitting in the aisle seat across from me. She looks at me with a knowing eye, and any loitering doubts vanish. She sees it: just as some potent of human life grows in her pale, gourd-like belly, so in me grows a huge and terrible blend of mold and rust. But all is well, I tell myself, channeling the wisdom of the Mantra-of-the-Month club I've subscribed to, and my self-help books-on-tape. Even if this pregnant girl has caught my indiscrete bout of consumption, I am the center of my universe. And who, really, is she?

After a few months I stopped thinking about my gerbil incident, and was reminded of it only by my mother's sporadic bouts of shame, and by the little white teeth that appeared in the toilet bowl well into the fifth grade. I told no one about the fantastic daydream that had sent my mind into ether that afternoon: I was on an airplane, flying first class, dressed as African royalty. Africa! Africa, of the capital A and the small a, and all the delicious unknown in between. My robes were heavenly, intricately swirled with Benin gold and deep purple, and there were large men and a frenzied air of camera flash around me. The sky was creamy yellow with thick, frothy clouds, several of which looked delicious. I remember now the excitement that had begun to sweep over me, before I was torn from that daydream by LaSharia Bennett's shrieks of horror at my fur-fuzzed face and shirt.

Since then, I have eaten many things. Telephone cords, fire hoses, nearly anything you would find lining the ground of Adam Clayton Powell Jr. Boulevard. And I have learned, with the help of my dear mother, to eat furtively and cover my tracks. It is amazing what gluttony you can get away with, you know, with just a little tact and creative thinking. Last week, for example, my good friend Patrice, who owns a brownstone in Bed-Stuy, invited me over for a barbecue. As I stood in line for a low-cal veggie burger, I was seized by the desire to hang glide. And then I *was* hang gliding, grip tight on thick black handlebars, my face and feet lifted and battered by air. It was a fabulous feeling, one that I was truly sad to let go of, and perhaps I would have stayed in that daydream longer, had I not gotten a splinter in my throat from the picket fence I had begun to munch on. I had eaten two long planks and was holding a third in my hand, but the pain of the splinter was so huge that I had to abandon my eating and hang gliding to find some water. Now, Patrice is the type who drinks tap water. And, well, you never know what's in the water these days, so I refuse to touch the stuff. Anyhow, Patrice didn't have any bottled water (she doesn't even own a Brita!), so it was iced tea for me. I knew that it would take at least a gallon to dislodge the wood from my throat and wash it down to a less delicate part of my GI tract, but the iced tea was loaded with sugar (Patrice has never had a weight problem) and I really did not want to ruin my diet, so I followed my grandmother's advice for swallowed fish bones, soaking a piece of bread in the tea and swallowing it whole. In the end I was happy to have rid myself of the splinter, and while I was disappointed with my behavior (carbs are not on my diet), I was able to pass the whole incident off as a party trick (some clowns eat fire, I eat wood).

Things like that happen all the time, and by now I have learned the tricks of the trade. First, I stay away from all animals. No exceptions. My gerbil incident, and a few other carnivorous episodes shortly after, taught me that fat in one's mouth really does become fat on the hips, the thighs, the belly. And who needs that? Plus, I can eat so much more of other things, like, for example, paint, which has no calories or teeth. Also, another tip: it is very important to stay in the daydream for as long as possible, preferably until present company has begun to scream or cry, for if you stop at people's quizzical looks or quiet expressions of concern, you will have eaten practically nothing, and you will miss the best part of the daydream. Finally, you must allow yourself to trust in the empathy and human kindness of your audience. For instance, after my gerbil incident, my mother nearly disowned me. But once I gave animals up in favor of other less fattening, synthetic items, I dropped fifty pounds, and her love for me increased tenfold. Such was the case with Patrice and her guests, too, and now that I am thin and famous I can tell you with certainty that people will tolerate almost any strange behavior as long as you don't eat too much food.

Still, I am embarrassed at times like these, when I seem to have ingested something so unappealing as an anvil in so public a space as this, and with cameras nearby. Had it been a magazine, an air mask, or even some of the cotton that is peeking coyly from the hole in the seat in front of me (in first class!), it would not be so bad. The pregnant lady would not be staring at me, her blonde eyebrows arched in shock. But I'm absolutely sure now that it was an anvil, because when I press here on my pelvic bone I feel a sharp protrusion. Yes, it was an anvil, and the pregnant girl looks as though she might faint at the sight of me. But no matter, really. I am on my way to Africa where I will be regarded as royalty, and when she sees me on television she will remember me with forgiveness and regret.

Wall Women

"Women have sat indoors all these millions of years, so that by this time, the very walls are permeated by their creative force, which has, indeed so overcharged the capacity of bricks and mortar that it must needs harness itself to pens and brushes and business and politics."
– Virginia Woolf

Women curve themselves around the television screen, whipping their hair against their backs, smacking it over bare shoulders, bending low and shaking it at their knees. The beat is steady and they seem steady too, always the same, always the same, like identical parts in a moving machine. But there is always one who catches my eye, throws the beat off, just a little. Today her hair is yellow. Not blonde, or gold. Not a color I've seen on heads before. It is crayon-yellow, the color of the sun in the pictures on the social workers' offices, drawn by the younger foster children, taped to the walls you sit under while you wait to go from one life to the next.

These same women are on every television screen—not just at the social workers' offices, but at the homes, too, even the new one where I am now. This home is different from all the others. I have been to four by now, two per year since I turned ten the year before last. Most of the houses are loud with children and always smell like food, but here there are no children here besides me. The woman here, my newest mother, has never brought children in before. "I'm surprised we got you," she tells me. "They never would've given you to me alone. Must be because of Obette."

While the crayon woman dances on TV, the mother, Cheryl, talks about Obette. She says Obette is the responsible one, the clear-headed one, the one with the good job and the plans. She says Obette has taken care of her, and soon she will take care of us both. Cheryl stirs grits at the stove and says that Obette will come back soon. She says Obette will love me, that she'll be so glad I'm here, and the three of us will be a pack.

Cheryl tells me about the dreams she has, and I'm not sure what kind she means at first—nighttime dreams or day. After a while, though, I know she means the better kind, the kind you can hold in your hand as long as you stay asleep. The other dreams— the day kind—are far away, like planets or imaginary friends. To me, sleeping dreams are better; they are all the way real, right up until they're not.

Cheryl tells me that, when she wakes up in the mornings, she does not know where she is, how things work. She thinks people can move without touching the ground, or that her mother is holding her hand. She tells me she does not know what world is real until she sees Obette beside her. Then she settles into herself like bubbles into a pan of dishwater, and they can begin the day.

I listen and do not say anything. I catch words here and there and mix them in my juice glass. *Pack, hand, ground, mother.* I wonder about the crayon woman, if she speaks, what she does when she is not dancing behind a screen. I wonder if she has someone like this Obette, someone who helps her settle into herself. Sometimes, I imagine myself dancing like her, a little out of step, my hair a neon shock on top of my head. But then I think about what other people would say about me—the social workers, the kids at the school, my next mother, whenever my next life comes. So I sit by the screen, I watch and I listen.

It never smells like food here, even though we eat fine every day. Mostly it smells like a woman working hard to build things—smells like paint and metal and wood and cinnamon tea. Every day, Cheryl talks and works on the house, sawing things, bringing in pretty lighting fixtures that she says Obette will like. She tells me her plans for the house, how the two of them will sleep in the big room upstairs and my room will be the one right next door. I don't wonder why they would share a room until Cheryl asks if I'm wondering. I shake my head and say, "No, it makes sense to me." I think for a second what my past mothers would say about it, but then I think, *How much can they matter, if they aren't here?*

Cheryl tells me we'll all play games and dance together in the back room, but the front room will be just for Obette. "She's like a man, but better," Cheryl says. "Time alone is how she keeps her magic."

I listen and watch the television, and then I go to the new school and I wait. Sometimes I'm waiting for someone to come—a police officer, a social worker—

219

and take me to my next life. Sometimes I'm just waiting for the day to end. One time I try to wait for Obette, like Cheryl has been doing since I came here, but I don't know how. A new life usually comes, the day always ends, but people are harder to wait for.

Soon I figure out that Cheryl is nice, and sad. I don't know how she takes my silence. Sometimes I think that she likes how I listen. The dead space between her talking gets shorter and shorter, and I think that if I wanted to I could leave the house and go dance on the corner while she talks, do all the dances the video women do, and then come back to find her right there, still talking, just fine. But in the end, I wouldn't want to go outside. I wouldn't know anyone, and no one wants to know a girl who dances by herself.

Soon, I start to like Cheryl. I like the stories she tells me about all the places she and Obette have been, all the things they have done together, and the things we will do, the pack of us, when Obette comes back. Soon, I stop waiting to leave. I stay and make Obette up in my mind, mix her in with the video women, only the strange ones, the ones with sad faces or candy hair.

"She'll be here tomorrow," Cheryl says one day after she picks me up from the school. I am watching a video, but I turn to her and listen. "Or maybe sometime next week. Obette is afraid," she says. "And fear slows people down. Do you understand?" But she doesn't wait for my answer.

One day, in the summer, Cheryl's dream is about ducks. They are half real and half fake, she tells me, with dirty feathers and ugly voices, but perfect orange feet.

She tells me about their yellow color, how it's bright but tinged with gray. She thinks they could fly, she says, because one of them, the biggest one, said something like that to her in the dream. "There were three of them, but then there were six," she says, "and sometimes they were all just one. And when they were one they were Obette. They smelled like soup, the way she smells when her body is working hard." And this makes Cheryl feel she should never wake up from the dream.

While she tells me this, she is frying sausages in a pan. She waves the spatula around, and I wonder if it will drip grease into the fire. Then I notice that I am afraid, and Cheryl is not. She presses the sausages into the pan and smoke puffs up, thick and almost blue. The grease makes a smear on the white wall that Cheryl has just painted. I worry that the house will burn down, that me and Cheryl and all the dreams will float away into ash. The smoke alarm goes off, but Cheryl just looks at me. I decide that I will cook from now on.

Later in the summer it gets hot and there is too much time to spend it all just waiting. Most summers, there is something new—a new mother or another child in the house, or some kind of problem. But this summer there is just me and Cheryl, going grocery shopping and making trips to the hardware store. Cheryl does all kinds of things to the house. She makes new banisters with ends that curl like thick wooden snakes and stains them in what she says is the color of Obette's palms. She buys putty and scrapes it along the bottoms of the walls, then presses long cylinders of wood into it so the cracks between the wall and the floor disappear. "Obette likes things to be seamless," she says, and I don't think I know what she means, but I nod.

On the day she paints the front room—Obette's room—Cheryl spends an hour standing in the middle of the floor, frowning. "It's not right," she says. "The walls are too flat for her." Again, I'm not sure I know what she means.

While she works I watch the video women dance behind the glass, and I make a game of counting the ones I will like. I follow the rhythm while I wait for Kool-Aid hair, a set of green fingernails, or a pair of talking eyes to flash across the screen. There is always noise outside the house. Children from the school are listening to music, doing all the dances, rapping and singing and tagging the stoops. I would not say this to anyone, but sometimes I do imagine myself with them. Sometimes, when Cheryl talks about Obette—all the thing she has done and the things we will do, the three of us—I get a feeling that I could dance with the kids, that they might not bother me for not talking, that I might not have to fight girls to tell them who I am, to prove I belong here, in this life. Other times, when Cheryl talks, I am afraid I am like her, and then I want to run hard and fast, through the plaster and the brick, to get out. But I don't want to leave Cheryl talking alone to the walls. And, also, I like her dreams. If I left, I would be alone, too, and I would miss them.

One morning, while I'm cooking, I hear Cheryl's voice loud in her bedroom. I turn the flame off and go quietly to her door. She has pushed the bed to the middle of the room and is cooing like a dying bird. When she sees me she begs me to help her.

"I can't move," she says.

She calls me Obette and tells me all of her dreams over again, all the ones I've heard already and new ones, too. She crawls over the mattress and kicks the sheets to the floor. She tells me that she needs me.

When I don't speak, she says, "Fuck you!" Her eyes tell me that in this dream she could tear a body apart. But when she moves to the edge of the bed, she shrieks like she's been shocked, then she whimpers and lies down. "Come back, please. Please."

On my way down the stairs I think of what to do. I think of the people I should go to—a social worker or a police officer, a teacher at the school or the nice man at the corner store—but I am afraid I will not know what to say. By the time my hand curves around the banister's tail, my voice is gone already. I feel like my mouth has melted away and all I am is limbs. My legs carry me into the front room, Obette's room. I step over the newspaper and the plastic tarps, the nails and the hammer and the cans of paint.

I feel strange, light, like I'm not sure where the ground is. I wonder if this is how Cheryl feels when she wakes up, if this is why she thinks only in dreams. My hands go soft and they sink toward the paint cans, pry them open. At first I don't know what I'm doing. I'm scared, but then I'm excited, my whole body filled with breath. I dip into the yellow and feel my fingers soak in the cool of the paint. Then I am at the wall, making smears that turn to yellow balls, and balls that turn to tufts of yellow fuzz, and fuzz that turns to feathers. I am painting ducks for Cheryl, hoping this will help her. Time disappears into Cheryl's voice as I fill the room with round yellow bodies, sculpting sloped heads and pulling perked tails up toward the ceiling. I run down the hall for the orange paint, and then I make long open beaks and webbed feet that float along the room's white sky. I am whirling, making ducks, Cheryl's ducks, no one else's. But when I look at them I see the yellow, and it makes *me* feel good, too. I feel like I am dancing in my own way, waiting for nothing, for no one. And so I keep going, my body bright and whirling in color, flying in its own directions, bouncing against nothing but air.

As I walk up the stairs, I can feel things bubbling in me. I put my hands in my hair, and I don't worry about the color I have left there. When I open the door, Cheryl is sleeping. She smiles when she feels me coming toward her.

"Obette?" she says.

I tell her "no," but I say it softly. Then I say my name.

Acknowledgments

These stories come from years of listening to and learning from many wonderful storytellers, advice-givers, coconspirators and supports. The first of these have been my parents, Martha and Jamal, who taught me early on to love books and value my imagination, and my brother, Malik, one of the smartest writers I know.

I am so fortunate to have had such a fabulous team of people collaborating on this project. I'm incredibly grateful to Magnus editor Don Weise, and Riverdale Avenue books publisher, Lori Perkins, whose time and care with this book have been invaluable, and to my agent, Janet Silver, from whose brilliance and generosity I learn new things with every step.

Thanks to the many teachers who have pushed me to pursue my writing to its best possible ends: Amy Kissell, Nancy Gannon, Daniel Rouse, Kevin Quashie, Suzanne Gauch, Salamishah Tillet, Heather Love, Herman Beavers, and Thadious Davis, who have shown me what it is to teach and learn from literature. And to the incredible writers whose encouragement and rich critique have made these stories better: Cheryl Clarke, Howard Norman, Randall Kenan, Jim Sheppard, Percival Everett, and especially Joan Mellen, Chip Delany, and Darryl Pinckney, whose time, thoughtfulness, and support over the years have meant everything.

This book wouldn't have been possible without the support of the Bread Loaf Writers' Conference, the National Endowment for the Arts, Yaddo, the Hedgebrook Writers' Retreat, the Pan-African Literary Forum in Ghana, the Hambidge Center, the New York State Summer Writers' Institute, and the Center for Fiction, whose incredible vision and tireless staff—especially Noreen Tomassi and Kristin Henley—have been nothing short of gifts for me. Thank you to the department of English at the University of Pennsylvania, the Women's, Gender, Sexuality Studies department at Williams College, the English department at Temple University, the English department at Rutgers University, and all of my colleagues in Women, Gender, Sexuality Studies at the University of Massachusetts, Amherst, for providing the best kinds of intellectual homes, and for supporting me in this project, and in all of my work. I'm grateful also for the resources at the Beinecke Rare Book and Manuscript Library at Yale University,

One of the best things about writing is that it puts you in touch with a world of writer friends. I'm grateful to all those who've read drafts, offered comments, and clinked glasses in joy and commiseration through the writing and rewriting: Quincy Scott Jones, Kamilah Aishah Moon, Rachel Eliza Griffiths, Kristen-Page Madonia, Aracelis Girmay, Marie-Helene Bertino, Kaitlyn Greenidge, Xoaquima Diaz, LaMonda Horton-Stallings, Marci Blackman, Tiphanie Yanique, and so many more. Thank you to my homies—my family of the heart—who have supported me and my dreams since forever:

Erica Khan, Keisha Warner, Nicole S. Junior, Lecynia Swire, Julia Jarcho, Ásta Hostetter, LaMarr Jurelle Bruce, and Effie Richardson, my fellow foodie, long-distance roommate, and middle-school kindred soul. Thank you to Patreese Johnson, Terrain Dandridge, Venice Brown, Renata Hill, Chenese Loyal, Lania Daniels, and Khamysha Coates for your fierceness and your courage. Thank you, Jeanette Aycock, for showing me what love and support look like, for years and years and years. C. Riley Snorton, thank you for being a true homie and showing me new depths of laughter; hope to see you on the AC soon. Nina Sharma, Fufs, the world's finest writer friend—and one of its greatest souls—your generosity and perceptiveness astound me every time; these stories owe so much to you.

And to Hanifah Walidah, the beautiful one, who has been down for me in every sense, supporting and loving me since the beginning in ways that have known no bounds—and to everyone I haven't named whose voices move through these pages—thank you, thank you, thank you.

If you liked this, look for more from Riverdale Avenue Books

Growing up Golem
How I Survived my Mother, Brooklyn, and Some Really Bad Dates
By Donna Minkowitz

http://riverdaleavebooks.com/books/3085/growing-up-golem-how-i-survived-my-mother-brooklyn-and-some-really-bad-dates

Confessions of a Librarian
A Memoir of Loves
by Barbara Foster

http://riverdaleavebooks.com/books/5160/confessions-of-a-librarian-a-memoir-of-loves

The Circlet Treasury of Lesbian Erotic Science Fiction and Fantasy
by Cecilia Tan

http://riverdaleavebooks.com/books/25/the-circlet-treasury-of-lesbian-erotic-science-fiction-and-fantasy

50 Shades of Pink
by KT Grant

http://riverdaleavebooks.com/books/5164/50-shades-of-pink